SCRAPBOOK STORIES

SCRAPBOOK STORIES

from

Ellen G. White's Scrapbooks

Selected by
ERNEST LLOYD

Illustrated by Frank McMillan

TEACH Services, Inc.
PUBLISHING
www.TEACHServices.com • (800) 367-1844

Copyright © 2005 TEACH Services, Inc.
ISBN-13: 978-1-57258-323-8 (Paperback)
Library of Congress Control Number: 2004118388

TEACH Services, Inc.
PUBLISHING
www.TEACHServices.com • (800) 367-1844

Contents

	PAGE
Listen, Boys and Girls	7
Joe Benton's Coals of Fire	13
Selling a Birthright	18
Mattie's Prize	20
Annie's Handy Box	24
School Sickness	26
Keeper of the Light	29
Florie's Birthday Party	33
The Hard Way	38
Rose's Revenge	42
Aunt Jane's Party	45
Into the Sunshine	47
Lily May's "Good Time"	49
Paul's Canary	52
Bertha's Queer Graveyard	57
The Boy Who Took a Boarder	62
One Minute More	66
Making Up	69
Joe Green's Lunch	71
The Conductor's Mistake	75
Burned Without Fire	78
The Temptation	83
The Two Gardens	88
Always the Bible	92

DEAR BOYS AND GIRLS:

Many years ago it was my privilege to spend a few months at Ellen G. White's home close to the St. Helena Sanitarium in California. It is known as "Elmshaven." A little office building stood near the home where Elder W. C. White and his helpers carried on the work of preparing Mrs. White's writings for publication. He was Mrs. White's son and had general charge of her affairs. I was one of Elder W. C. White's helpers.

During my stay at "Elmshaven," Elder W. C. White gave me two old scrapbooks that his mother had compiled with her own hands. In the early years of her work, though a busy woman, she took time to gather up the best stories she could find for boys and girls. While absent from her home on long trips, papers would accumulate. She would often find relaxation in reading and clipping the stories and pasting them in the scrapbooks. Other stories that Mrs. White gathered found their way into the *Golden Grains* booklets and *Sabbath Readings for the Home Circle,* which, no doubt, some of your fathers and mothers read when they were your age.

I have selected and edited the best scrapbook stories and put them into this new book for you. They are stories that never grow old, and they are helpful to boys and girls. I believe you will enjoy the stories and will lend this book for others to enjoy.

Yours for more good storybooks in every home,

ERNEST LLOYD.

(6)

Listen, Boys and Girls

WHEN I was a boy in knee pants, and very much given to reading, my father and mother bought for my brothers and sisters and me four little books of stories, called *Sabbath Readings*. They had been gathered together and published by a woman whom we knew as Ellen White. Some of those stories have stayed in my memory and helped me over hard places for many years. I don't know who wrote all those stories, but I do know that Mrs. White thought they were good for boys and girls, and so do I.

Elder and Mrs. White had some boys of their own. They had no girls, though at times they took other girls and boys to live in their home and these were like their own children. It was for all these that Mrs. White first gathered the stories. Then she thought about the boys and girls in the families all over the land and in the churches who would also be happy to read such stories. That is how she came to have them printed in books.

Well, here are some stories that Mrs. White gathered. She put them in scrapbooks—more stories than could go into the printed books. The stories in the printed books came out of the scrapbooks, but there were some scrapbooks left over. One of her boys, Willie, whom your fathers knew as W. C. White, kept these scrapbooks until he was an old man; then he gave them to Elder Lloyd, who thought it would be a good plan to publish some of them. So did the Pacific Press, and here they are in this book.

Now imagine you were Elder and Mrs. White's little boy or girl ninety years ago, or imagine that you were in my family seventy years ago, and we shall go sailing together on the seas of story land.

Stories, you know, fit the time in which they were written. These stories are different from stories of the time in which we live. You'd hardly know yourself if you should suddenly be

(7)

taken back to a hundred years ago. Certainly any boys and girls who lived then, if they had been picked up and taken into our times, would have wondered what world they were in.

For one thing, they talked differently; at least in books they talked differently. Oh, they used words you know, though you know some words they didn't know, because new things have come into being, and new names with them. But they tried to be very proper—no short cuts like "'twould" and "we'll" and "can't;" they said, "it would" and "we will" and "cannot." They dressed differently, a bit, though not so differently as the Bible folks dressed long ago. Every age is strange to every other. If you had seen me in the copper-toed shoes I was so proud of (couldn't wear 'em out, you know!), or if you had seen my sisters with their red knitted wool stockings and their balloon sleeves—well, anyway, it doesn't do to laugh at anyone, because we look as queer to them as they do to us. We're all poor mortals!

Life was different in some ways from what it is now. For instance, there were no automobiles then. If you wanted to go anywhere, you walked or rode horseback or traveled in a buggy or a wagon. The roads were all dirt roads outside the big cities, and even in them many streets were not paved. Oh, what clouds of dust in dry weather, or mud puddles in wet weather! People used to wear "dusters," long, thin linen coats, buttoned up to the chin; and when they reached their journey's end, they would shake off all the dust they could, and then scrub up. In rainy weather they rode, if they could, in closed carriages or covered wagons; but sometimes they had to get out and help the horses pull the wagon out of the mudholes.

There were some other ways to travel, to be sure. There were the railway trains, with short wooden cars that had wooden seats. They were quite new in our country then. People thought they were wonderful, and they really were. They kept on improving until now they are luxury cars. Then there were boats on the rivers, lakes, and seas. There had been steamboats twice as long a time as there had been railway trains; so some of these boats had grown to be more comfortable than the cars, and they were very good to travel on, if so be they went where you wanted to go.

Another kind of boat used a great deal was the canalboat. Canals, you know, are waterways like rivers which men dig between two greater bodies of water, and then turn the water in. They made long, narrow, shallow boats for these canals. To make a canalboat go, they hitched a team of mules or horses to it, and drove the team along the bank, or towpath, to draw the boat. Some of these boats carried freight; some of them, called "line boats," carried both passengers and light freight; and the best, called "packets," carried only people. The most famous of these waterways was the Erie Canal, between the Hudson River and Lake Erie. Before they had railroads, the Erie Canal carried most of the freight and the passengers from East to West and West to East.

The automobile is only one of the things they did not have then which make a different kind of world. For instance, there was no electricity, either for lighting houses or for driving machines. At night, people made light by fires in their fireplaces, or by wax or tallow candles, or by oil lamps. These oil lamps burned whale oil, though about that time they did begin to use kerosene. And didn't they think kerosene, or coal oil, lamps were fine! They were, too. You could see by them many times better than by candle or by firelight. But nothing like electric lights. Sometimes in our house now, if the electric current goes off, we get out a kerosene lamp, and how we squint to try to read by it!

Airplanes? Why, people were so far from having airplanes that they joked about the idea of men flying. We had a poem when I was a boy that poked fun at "D'rius Green and his flyin' machine." It told of a boy named Darius who secretly made a flying machine up in the loft of the shed, and when all the folks had gone to town for a Fourth-of-July celebration, he tried it out. He tied its wings to his arms, jumped off, and tried to flap the wings; but he came tumbling down, broke the machine all to pieces, and bruised himself up. And he—

> Stanched his sorrowful nose with his cuff.
> "Wal, I like flyin' well enough,"
> He said, "but the' ain't sich a thunderin' sight
> O' fun in't when ye come to light!"

We thought men never would fly until they became like the angels. Now, of course, nearly everyone flies sometimes, and we think no more of it than we used to think of going to town once a month. You can fly from New York to San Francisco in half a day, where men used to take more than a week to go by the fastest train, and before that they took three or four months to go by ox team.

No telephones; though they did have the telegraph, just then invented. But radio! Why, to think of men talking through the air, thousands of miles, was even more foolish than to think of men flying! No phonographs, either, nor moving pictures. There were newspapers, and some magazines, and books—all the books you could read or pay for. Here and there was a free library, but only here and there. If you went to the city, you could actually see streetcars, drawn by mules; but who would want, when he had two good feet, to pay a nickel to ride, except maybe only once to see what it felt like?

If you lived on a farm in those days you worked; I'll tell you, you worked. Well, work is good for everyone, and it made sturdy boys and girls, who grew up into worth-while men and women. There were delights for the country boy and girl that hardly anyone nowadays knows or takes time to sample: same good old sun rising every morning on a dewy world, raindrops sparkling like diamonds, or snow blanket promising snowball fights and coasting and sleighing; swimming hole in the bend of the creek under the elm trees—beat your tiled swimming pool all hollow; mayflowers, violets, strawberries in the spring, rattlesnake watermelons in the summer, spicy apples in the fall—snow, Northern Spy, Baldwin, sheepnose; pumpkins! jack-o'-lanterns, pumpkin pies, cranberry sauce, and so on, Thanksgiving!

The country boy was born, so to speak, with a hoe in his hand, and the country girl with a milk pail and a wooden spoon. No milking machine then, nor cream separator, no tractor with a gang plow, no reaper or mowing machine. Father hitched old Charley to the cultivator, and Jack and Dan followed with hoes, to keep the weeds down. Mother skimmed the milk, down in the springhouse, and Sarah Ann pumped that old churn handle until the butter came. Harvesttime, men went out into the field with scythes and cradles, and reaped the wheat; girls, maybe mother, came behind and bound the sheaves; father and boys threshed it out on the barn floor with flails, winnowed it in the wind, stored it in the granary alongside the corncrib to be filled to the eaves with husked yellow corn. Oh, it would take a book to tell you all we did on the farm. Very few machines to do our work. Of course there was the gristmill up the creek, with its great water wheel, where we ground our wheat and corn. At home there was the cider press—m-m-m—good sweet cider, popcorn, blueberries and milk and graham bread!

Well, that was the world that Elder and Mrs. White lived in, a hundred years ago and some less. He was born in 1821, and she was born in 1827. They were married in 1846, which is only a little more than a century back. Then they lived and worked on for the years that followed, through the many changes that came in people's lives and in all the world. Elder White died in 1881, but Mrs. White lived until 1915, a very old lady. Still, you could not remember that far back, for it is now thirty-five years ago, and I know you are not that old.

God gave them a great work to do. They were young people when they began to tell the world of Jesus' soon coming and the Sabbath and all the truths that go with them. Elder White was a great preacher and writer and publisher. He loved the children and the young people. He started *The Youth's Instructor,* and the Review and Herald Publishing Association where it is printed. He founded the Pacific Press, where *Our Little Friend* and this book are published for the children.

Ellen White was by his side as long as he lived. She taught temperance and healthful living, she taught fathers and mothers how to train their children, she worked and prayed for people little and great, and rejoiced when they took Jesus for their Saviour. She wrote many books. She always worked hard and faithfully and beautifully and nobly, to the day of her death. She loved the Bible, and she loved nature, the handbook of God. One time I was with her out in her garden. She was eighty-five years old then; but she loved to walk in the midst of her flowers and shrubs and trees, and talk with God. We came to a beautiful bed of pansies, those flowers that almost seem to have human faces. Mrs. White knelt down by them, that dear old lady, and as she fingered their blossoms, she murmured: "The smiles of God! the smiles of God!"

Elder and Mrs. White traveled all over the United States, preaching and teaching. In the early days that travel was not easy. They had little money, and they traveled as cheaply as they could. Sometimes they drove with horse and buggy, or two horses and a carriage. Sometimes they traveled by canalboat, sometimes by steamboat, sometimes on the train. Often they were sleepless, often in peril; but God delivered them out of all dangers and gave them strength to keep on with their work. After Elder White died, Mrs. White not only worked in America, but crossed the seas to Europe and to Australia, where she lived for many years. But always she was writing, writing, teaching, teaching, lifting up the old people and the young people and the children.

The family loved to sing together. They had beautiful voices, and they knew by heart the grand old hymns and the sweet simple songs of home and childhood. The boys, as they grew older, learned to play the organ,—they couldn't afford a piano,—and the music of their voices and instrument made the morning and evening worshiptimes, and all the day, happy.

So she loved them and cared for them. She sewed their clothes, and she cooked their food, and she nursed them when they were sick, and she taught them their manners, and she told them stories, and she prayed with them, and she lifted them up toward manhood. The scrapbooks that she made were one of the many ways that she planned to help them become good men. I imagine those books were popular in their home. When mother had to go away and be gone long, and the house was lonesome, even with the good help and cheer that Clarissa and Frances and Mary gave, I think the boys must often have taken the scrapbooks, with the good stories in them, and said, as they read together: "This is mother's book!" So the stories in the scrapbooks helped them, as they helped me, and as I am sure they are going to help you. God bless you, boys and girls!   ARTHUR W. SPALDING.

Joe Benton's Coals of Fire

IT WAS a lovely morning; the sun was shining brightly, and the air was fragrant with violets and lilacs when Joe Benton sprang out the back door, shouting for joy over the anticipated pleasures of the holiday. "I'll have time to run to the brook before breakfast and see if my boat is all right," he said to himself. "We boys are to meet and launch her at nine o'clock, and the captain ought to be up on time."

So Joe hastened down to the cave where the precious boat was hidden. As he neared the place, an exclamation of surprise escaped him. There were signs of some intruder, and the big stone before the cave had been rolled away. Hastily drawing forth his treasure, he burst into loud cries of dismay; for there was the beautiful little boat which Cousin Herbert had given him, with its gay sails split into many shreds, and a large hole bored in the bottom.

Joe stood for a moment, motionless with grief and surprise; then, with a face as red as a peony, he burst forth: "I know who did it! It was Fritz Brown, and he was angry because I didn't ask him to come to the launching. But I'll pay him back for this," said Joe. Hastily pushing back the ruined boat, he went a little farther down the road. He fastened a piece of string across the footpath a few inches from the ground and carefully hid himself in the bushes.

Presently a step was heard, and Joe eagerly peeped out. How provoking! Instead of Fritz, it was Cousin Herbert, the last person he cared to see. Joe tried to lie very quiet; but it was all in vain. Cousin Herbert's sharp eyes caught a

As soon as *Fritz* saw *Joe*, he hurried to present to him a beautiful flag he had bought for the sailboat with part of his egg money.

curious movement in the bushes, and, brushing them right and left, he soon came upon Joe. "How's this?" cried he, looking straight into the boy's face; but Joe answered not a word. "You're not ashamed to tell me what you were doing?"

"No, I'm not," said Joe sturdily, after a short pause. "I'll tell you the whole story." Out it tumbled, down to the closing threat. "I mean to make him smart for it," said Joe.

"What do you mean to do?"

"You see, Fritz carries a basket of eggs to the store every morning, and I plan to trip him over this string, and make him smash all of them."

Now Joe knew well enough that he was not showing the right spirit, and he muttered to himself, "Now for a good scolding;" but to his great surprise Cousin Herbert said quietly: "Well, I think Fritz does need some punishment; but this string is an old trick. I can tell you something better than that."

"What?" cried Joe eagerly.

"How would you like to put a few coals of fire on his head?"

"What, and burn him?" said Joe doubtfully.

Cousin Herbert nodded with a queer smile.

Joe clapped his hands. "Now that's just the thing, Cousin Herbert. You see, his hair is so thick he wouldn't get burned much before he'd have time to shake them off; but I'd like to see him jump once. Tell me how to do it, quick!"

" 'If thine enemy be hungry, give him bread to eat; and if he be thirsty, give him water to drink: for thou shalt heap coals of fire upon his head, and the Lord shall reward thee,' " said Cousin Herbert gravely. "I think that's the best kind of punishment Fritz could have."

Joe's face lengthened terribly. "Now, that's no punishment at all."

"Try it once," said Cousin Herbert. "Treat Fritz kindly, and I am certain that he will feel so ashamed and unhappy he would far rather you had given him a severe beating."

Joe was not really a bad boy at heart; but he was now in an ill temper, and he said sullenly: "You said this kind of coals would burn, and they don't at all."

"You're mistaken about that," said his cousin cheerily. "I have known such coals to burn up a great amount of rubbish—malice, envy, ill feeling, revenge, and I don't know how much more—and then leave some cold hearts feeling as warm and pleasant as possible."

Joe drew a long sigh. "Well, tell me a good coal to put on Fritz's head, and I'll see about it."

"You know," said Herbert, smiling, "Fritz is poor and he can seldom buy himself a book, although he loves to read. Now you have quite a library. Suppose—ah, well, I won't suppose anything about it! I'll leave you to find your own coal; but be sure to kindle it with love, for no other fire burns so brightly and so long." With a cheery "good-by," Herbert sprang over the fence and was gone.

Before Joe had time to collect his thoughts, he saw Fritz coming down the lane with a basket of eggs in one hand and a pail of milk in the other.

For one moment, the thought crossed Joe's mind: "What a smash it would have made if Fritz had fallen over the string!" Then he stopped, glad that the string was safe in his pocket.

Fritz looked uncomfortable when he first caught sight of Joe; but the boy began abruptly: "Fritz, have you much time to read now?"

"Sometimes," said Fritz, "when I've driven the cows home, and done all my work; but the trouble is, I've read everything I can get hold of."

"How would you like to take my new book of travels?"

Fritz's eyes danced. "Say, would you let me? I'd be careful with it!"

"Yes," answered Joe, "and perhaps I've some others you'd like to read." Then he added shyly: "Fritz, I would ask you to come and help sail my boat today; but someone has torn up the sails, and made a hole in the bottom. Who do you suppose did it?"

Fritz's head dropped, but after a moment he looked up, and said: "I did it, Joe; but I can't begin to tell you how sorry I am. You did not know I was so mean when you promised me the books."

"Well, I rather thought you did it," said Joe slowly.

"And yet you—" Fritz couldn't get any further. He rushed off without another word.

"That coal does burn. I know Fritz would rather I had smashed every egg in his basket than to have offered him that book." Then Joe went home with a light heart, hungry for his breakfast.

When the captain and the crew of the little vessel met at the appointed hour, they found Fritz there before them trying to repair the damage. As soon as he saw Joe, he hurried to present him with a beautiful little flag he had bought for the boat with part of his egg money that morning. The boat was repaired, and everything turned out as Herbert had said. Joe found that the more he used of this curious kind of coal, the larger supply he had on hand—kind thoughts, kind words, and kind actions.

Joe's playmates, who saw that he was always happy, studied the secret, and when any trouble came up, someone would say: "Let us try a few of Joe Benton's coals." It was astonishing to see how quickly their hearts grew warm toward each other.

Selling a Birthright

"FATHER," said Charley one day, "Mr. Reed is going to take the whole school to Union Hill, where we are to have a dinner and a grand time. We are to choose a captain from the senior class."

"Whom are you going to vote for in the election?"

"Morton, the tallest fellow in school, and the best boy, too, I think. But George has gone over to the opposition."

Father looked at George. "Who is your candidate? Let's hear about it."

"Chester is my choice," said George. "I don't see why he won't make as good a captain as Morton."

"He is not so good a scholar," said Charley. "Besides, he swears sometimes. Then, too, he's buying up votes, and I think that is mean."

George flushed a little, but made no reply.

"George," said his father, "I want you to tell me whether Chester has given you anything to influence your vote."

George hung his head and was slow to reply. There was no escape from his father's question, and at last he answered: "I broke my new bat yesterday playing baseball. George gave me his if I would promise to vote for him."

"Did you promise?"

"Yes, father."

"You were wrong, my boy. Your vote is your birthright. Not long ago, when we read how Esau sold his birthright for a mess of pottage, you thought him a foolish man. Now you have sold yours for a secondhand bat. You have sold your influence, as far as it goes, to vote for a boy who, by taking unfair means, shows he is unfit for the position. Now, as you look over the whole affair, do you not think that it is pretty cheap?"

"Yes," answered George; "but I didn't think it was so important."

"If you can be bought with a bat when you are a boy, you may be bought with an office, or with money, when you are a man. I want my sons to be above taking bribes or selling their freedom."

"What should I do?"

"Take the bat back to Chester and tell him how the matter looks to you on further consideration. If he has any honor in him, he will release you from your promise; if he has none, he can hold you to it, and you must keep your word. But take care not to be caught in such a position again."

George wished the old bat were at the bottom of the sea as he carried it back to Chester. He was laughed at, reproached, and held to his promise, as he expected to be; and acquired such a contempt for his candidate's lack of principle that he was glad when he found himself on the losing side the next day. In fact, he joined heartily in the cheers which the winners gave for their friend Morton.

Mattie's Prize

WHAT was Mattie turning over and over in her hand, looking admiringly at it the while? Every now and then a ripple of laughter broke from her lips. She was sitting on the floor in the front room, wishing mother would wake up to hear of her good fortune and help her admire this wonderful prize.

It would not do to awaken her, for she was getting over a long, severe sickness. Mattie, though only eight years old, knew that every hour of sleep was bringing her mother nearer to health again. Still, it was trying for her to sit quietly with such a wonderful thing to tell. She at last decided she could not wait any longer, and she went to find Aunt Fanny.

Aunt Fanny was getting dinner, but she looked up with a smile as Mattie put her rosy face in at the door.

"Is your mother still asleep, Mattie?" she asked.

"Yes. What did Dr. Morris say today?"

"He thinks she will soon be about again. He said it would do her a great deal of good to take a ride, but we must give that up."

"Why, Aunt Fanny?"

"Because we cannot spare the money. You know, dear, your mother's sickness not only keeps her from her students, but it takes many hours from her sewing. We shall have to live very economically for a long time to keep out of debt. So, you see, we cannot spare five dollars for a ride."

"Will it cost that much?"

"I tried my best, and when I had finished, the man said, 'This little girl has fairly earned the prize,' and he put in my hand a five-dollar bill."

"Yes, Mattie. It's no use to go for a little city drive. What your mother needs is a good breath of country or sea air, and it will take a long ride to get that. It is such a lovely afternoon, too," she added regretfully.

"Aunt Fanny, we will go. You get mamma ready, and I will make the arrangements. What time should we start?"

"It is nearly twelve. Say one o'clock," said Aunt Fanny as the little girl rushed off.

It was well for her that the invalid was awake when she returned, for her delightful news certainly would not keep much longer. Her mother was waiting as impatiently as Aunt Fanny for an explanation, and the happy child was eager to give it.

"We were all in school this morning, mother, when Miss Stratton told us that some great man—I did not catch his name—was going around the building to see how our school was managed. After a few minutes he came in with four or five other men. We went through some of the exercises and sang for him.

"Then he said: 'Now I want to hear some of the little girls read aloud. I will give this to the best reader.' And he held up something, I could not see what.

"Miss Stratton called up five girls to read, and I was among them. When it came my turn, mother, I remembered all you had told me about punctuation, distinctness, and expression, and I tried my best. I was the last, and when I finished he said, 'This little girl has fairly earned the prize,' and he put in my hand—see, mamma!"—and Mattie held out her treasure—"a five-dollar bill.

"I danced all the way home and found you asleep. Then I sat down and tried to think of all I could buy for five dollars. I wanted to run right out and get you some oranges and grapes and all sorts of good things. I wanted to buy you a new pair of slippers—yours are so shabby. I wanted to get you—"

"Stop, stop, little daughter! Did you not want to buy something for yourself with your five dollars?"

"Oh, mamma, I have everything I want!"

"I thought I heard a little girl wishing for a new hat and shoes."

"Oh, the old ones will do! Wouldn't I look nice," said Mattie scornfully, "buying myself hats and shoes, when you are sick! Well, I was trying to decide what to buy, and went to ask Aunt Fanny, and she told me about the good a ride would do you. So, mamma, we will go for a ride down to the seashore, and make you well and strong again."

"But, Mattie, it seems too bad to take your prize from you so soon."

"Too bad! As if I cared for the money half as much as I care to get you well! Besides, mother, if you had not taken so much pains to teach me to read well, I would never have had the prize. So, you see, it is really yours, after all. Now let me help Aunt Fanny dress you. Isn't it beautiful to see you have a hat on again!"

It would be quite beyond my power of description to give any idea of that ride. The best part of it, for the little girl, was the sight of a faint flush upon her mother's pale cheeks, a new light in her eyes, a stronger, clearer ring in her weak voice.

After happy, tired Mattie was fast asleep in her own little bed, the mother said: "I was downhearted, Fanny, thinking I must give up the struggle for health; but my little daughter's gift must be repaid by making every effort to get well again. I will get well for her sake."

"Yes, indeed," Aunt Fanny said heartily; "for there are not many little girls who would have no thought of self after winning such a prize."

Annie's Handy Box

"ONE of my glove buttons is gone," said sister Kate, as she was preparing to go out. "How provoking it is! A glove looks so untidy unfastened."

"Wait a minute, sis," said Annie, "I believe I have some glove buttons in my handy box." Opening it, she found a little tin box. She poured the contents in her apron and soon found the required button. Her handy needle and silk quickly sewed it on, and she was well repaid by a kiss from her sister. "Thank you, Annie," said Kate, "your little box of curiosities is a perfect gold mine. You can always find the right thing there." Down the steps she went, quite satisfied that all was right.

"How long have you had that box, Annie?" asked Ned, who was spending a week at the house.

"Ever since she can remember, I guess," said mother, laughing. "She always was careful about little things from the time she could toddle about the floor. She used to make collections of buttons and pretty stones when she was four years old. It is a good habit, though, and I am sure we are all indebted to her every day. It would be a curiosity to keep an account of the calls she has for her handy box."

"I think I will do it," said Ned. "Where can I find a paper and pencil?"

Annie opened her box again and took out the half of an old envelope she had saved, and a piece of pencil someone had swept out of doors.

"You can set down three things to begin with," she

said, laughing—"a glove button, piece of paper, and pencil."

Little Martha came running in holding the string from her cap. She was in "such a hurry."

"Run to Annie," said mother, who was busy making pies.

Up went the box lid, and this time a little bag containing all sorts of odds and ends of old strings and ribbons was inspected. The right thing was there, and, using a threaded needle, Annie sewed it on in a minute's time, and Martha went dancing off to her play.

"No. 4," said Ned, as father came in and asked Annie if she could find a strong piece of string. Another little bag was produced and it contained what was wanted. With a "Thank you, daughter, you are a treasure, and so is your box," he went on his way.

"Take your work and don't stir from that corner today," said Ned; "you'll be wanted. You might set up a store. Well, Tommy, what can we do for you?"

"I have lost my mitten, sister, and I can't make a snow man without it. May I have another?"

"Now, I think you are stuck, Annie," said Ned.

Annie smiled and said to Tommy: "If sister will give you another mitten' will you go and look for the lost one?"

The little fellow promised, and was told to go and warm his feet by the fire. Annie took out a paper pattern and a bit of thick cloth, which she quickly cut mitten shape and sewed up, all in fifteen minutes' time.

Ned looked on, dumb with admiration, and secretly resolved to learn a lesson.

Who else would like to have such a handy box? It is useful, not only to yourself, but to others. It will help to form the good habit of saving that which is valuable for use later on.

School Sickness

ONE morning Willie was attacked by a curious but common headache. He had been subject to such attacks before. They seemed worse just before schooltime, decreased rapidly toward noon, and appeared again about one o'clock. As they were growing upon him, mother desired to prevent the attacks in the future.

He was sitting in the big armchair, looking disconsolate, when his mother entered the room. "Come, Willie," said she, "you'll be late to school."

"Oh, mother, I have an awful headache, and I feel sick."

"Indeed! I'm sorry. I'll go and get my castor oil, and then put you to bed."

"Oh, I'm not sick enough to take medicine or go to bed," said Willie, looking a little brighter, but not entirely recovered.

"Well, then, I'll wrap you in my big shawl, and let you sit by the fire. You can study your lesson and recite to me."

"Don't you think it would do me good to run up and see Mr. Winters a little while, mother? I need the fresh air."

He looked longingly out through the open door, where the dog was dozing in the sunshine. The birds were singing, and everything seemed happy outside. But he was an invalid, confined to a warm kitchen. How he did wish he had gone to school! He had not thought his mother would take his plea of sickness so seriously.

"I can't study," he said at last, looking up. "All my books are at school. I didn't know I was going to be at home."

"You needn't worry, if that's all," said the mother. "I remember seeing my books in the attic a few days ago."

"I fear they're too old."

"I don't believe they are much different from the ones you use. I'll go up and look for them."

"Can't I go?" cried Willie eagerly, forgetting his headache.

"No, my dear, you might catch cold. Sit still."

So Willie settled back in his big chair, indeed looking much like an invalid.

While he was alone he could hear in the distance the voices of the children at play during recess. How he longed to be out playing.

When his mother came back with a spelling book, Willie's headache returned. He passed his morning twisting about in the chair and wishing for dinnertime to come. At noon, Johnny, one of his friends, came to see why he had been absent.

"It's nice to be a little sick. I wish I were," said the boy, gazing wistfully at Willie in the big chair.

"No, it's perfectly horrid. I will never be sick again."

"But when are you coming back to school?"

"This afternoon," cried Willie decidedly. "I mean to go to school all my life."

"You must not go to school this afternoon, son. You'll have to wait until you are well," said mother, determined to make a sure cure.

"Oh, mother, can't I go, please? I don't feel sick now."

Johnny, not understanding the situation, looked in amazement at Willie. He wished that his mother would act the same way when he didn't want to go to school.

Willie had a dreary afternoon and was glad when night

came. In the morning he was up bright and early. As soon as his mother appeared, he cried out: "I can go to school today, can't I, mother?"

"I'm afr—" began his mother.

Willie broke in: "Now, mother, I just must. I'll go crazy if I have to stay home another day."

"Well, then, you must wear your coat. You mustn't get sick again."

When Willie showed the slightest desire to stay away from school after that, his mother would say: "Willie, don't you feel well? You can stay at home with me today and rest, if you like." But the invitation has never yet been accepted. So far, Willie has carried out his intention not to miss school.

✳ Keeper of the Light

M ARY'S father was the keeper of a lighthouse on the coast of England. The light of these lamps shines at night to guide ships on their way and to keep them from dangerous rocks and shoals. The lighthouse seems to say: "Take care, sailors, for rocks and sands are here. Keep a good lookout and mind how you sail, or you will be lost."

One afternoon Mary was in the lighthouse alone. Mary's father had trimmed the lamps, and they were ready for lighting when evening came. As he needed to buy some food, he crossed the causeway which led to the land. This causeway was a path over the rocks and sands, which could be used only two or three hours in the day; at other times, the waters rose and covered it. The father intended to hasten home before the tide flowed over this path. Night was coming on, and a storm was rising on the sea. Waves dashed against the rocks, and the wind moaned around the tower.

Mary's mother was dead, and although she was alone, her father had told the girl not to be afraid, for he would soon return. Now there were some rough-looking men behind a rock, who were watching Mary's father. They watched him go to the land.

Who were they? They were "wreckers" who lurked about the coast. If a vessel was driven on the rocks by a storm, they rushed down—not to help the sailors, but to rob them, and to plunder the ship.

The wicked men knew that a little girl was left alone

Mary was alone in the dark lighthouse when the storm broke.

in the lighthouse. They planned to keep her father on the shore all night. Ships filled with rich goods were expected to pass the point before the morning and these men knew if the light did not shine, the vessels would run upon the rocks and be wrecked. How cruel and wicked they were to seek the death of the ships' crews!

Mary's father had filled his basket, and prepared to return to the lighthouse. As he drew near the road leading to the causeway, the wreckers rushed from their hiding place and threw him on the ground. They quickly bound his hands and feet with ropes and carried him into a shed, where he had to lie until morning. It was in vain that he shouted for them to set him free; they only mocked his distress. They then left him in the charge of two men, while they ran back to the shore.

"Oh, Mary, what will you do?" cried the father as he lay in the shed. "There will be no one to light the lamps. Ships may be wrecked, and sailors may be lost."

Mary looked from a narrow window toward the shore, thinking it was time for her father to return. When the clock in the little room struck six, she knew that the water would soon be over the causeway.

An hour passed. The clock struck seven, and Mary still looked toward the beach; but her father was not to be seen. By the time it was eight, the tide was nearly over the causeway; only bits of rock here and there were above the water. "O father, hurry," cried Mary, as though her father could hear her. "Have you forgotten your little girl?" But the only answer was the noise of the waters as they rose higher and higher, and the roar of the wind as it gave notice of the coming storm. Surely there would be no lights that night.

Mary thought of what her mother used to say: "We should pray in every time of need." Quickly she knelt and prayed for help: "O Lord, show me what to do, and bless my father, and bring him home safe."

The water was now over the causeway. The sun had set more than an hour ago, and, as the moon rose, black storm clouds covered it from sight.

The wreckers walked along the shore, looking for some ship to strike on the coast. They hoped that the sailors, not seeing the lights, would think they were far at sea.

At this moment Mary decided she would try to light the lamps. But what could a little girl do? The lamps were far above her reach. She got matches and carried a small stepladder to the spot. After much labor she found that the lamps were still above her head. Then she got a small table and put the stepladder on it. But when she climbed to the top the lights were still beyond her reach. "If I had a stick," she said, "I would tie a match to it, and then I could set a light to the wicks." But no stick was to be found.

The storm was raging with almost hurricane force. The sailors at sea looked along the coast for the light. Where could it be? Had they sailed in the wrong direction? They were lost and knew not which way to steer.

All this time Mary's father was praying that God would take care of his child in the dark and lonely lighthouse.

Mary, frightened and lonely, was about to sit down again, when she thought of the old Bible in the room below. But how could she step on that Book? It was God's Holy Word that her mother had loved to read. "Yet, it is to save life," said she; "and if mother were here, would she not allow me to take it?"

In a minute the large book was brought and placed under the steps, and up she climbed once more. Yes, she was high enough! She touched one wick, then another, and another, until the rays of the lamps shone brightly far above the dark waters.

The father saw the light as he lay in the shed, and thanked God for sending help in the hour of danger. The sailors saw the light, and steered their ships away from the rocks. The wreckers, too, saw the light, and were angry to see that their evil plot had failed.

All that stormy night the lamps cast their rays over the foaming sea; and when the morning came, the father escaped from the shed. Soon he reached the lighthouse and found out how his little girl had stood faithful to duty in the dark hours of storm.

Florie's Birthday Party

FLORIE SWIFT would be eight years old tomorrow, and her mother had promised her the company of six young friends to take dinner with her and spend the afternoon. "You may invite whom you please," mother said.

As soon as lessons were over, the girl went out, accompanied by Ann, the maid, to invite her guests. Ann thought, of course, that Florie would invite Fannie Morris, Jennie Snow, and two or three other close playmates. They lived in large houses on the next street, so Ann started to turn in that direction.

"Where are you going?" asked Florie. "The company I am going to invite don't live there. Those girls have many good times."

On they walked until they came to a narrow street with a none-too-inviting appearance.

"I am going to stop here," said Florie. She opened a rickety door and began to climb the stairs. Stopping at the top of the first flight, she knocked at the door on her right. "Come in," was faintly heard. Florie opened the door and found a girl about her own age sitting in a chair, knitting. This was Mary Gray, the daughter of a woman who had done sewing for Florie's mother. The child was blind, but she held out her hand in the direction of Florie's voice.

"Mrs. Gray," Florie said, "I came to see if you would allow Mary to have dinner with me tomorrow. It is my birthday, and mamma has promised me a little party. I will send for Mary, if you are willing."

(33)

Mrs. Swift greeted blind Mary, Amy, Tommy, and the other guests Florie had invited. It was a delightful party, and everyone had a happy time.

"How good you are, Miss Florie!" the woman replied. "My little child has but few pleasures. I know she will enjoy her visit with you."

"Thank you," said Mary, with a wan smile. "I'll be waiting for the party."

"I will send for you, Mary, at three o'clock tomorrow."

Bidding the mother and daughter good-by, Florie went down the stairs and hurried along to another house near by, where a large boot hung out for a sign. Ann looked at Florie in amazement as she entered this little shop. An old man sat mending shoes, and a little lame boy propped up in a chair was trying to amuse himself with some bits of bright-colored leather.

"Well, Miss Florie," exclaimed the child, "I am so glad you have come! Those roses you sent me a few days ago were so beautiful. I kept them as long as I could."

"I'm glad you liked them, Jamie. I have come to invite you to dinner tomorrow, and you shall have as many roses as you can carry home."

The little fellow glanced at his lame feet, and then at his crutches.

"Never mind, Jamie," the old shoemaker said. "I will carry you to Miss Florie's."

Florie now left for another home on a side street. She stopped at the door of a shabby-looking house, which was occupied by an old woman, formerly a nurse in Florie's family.

"Bless you, Miss Florie, it does me good to see your bright face," said the woman. "No one has been to read the story of the Good Shepherd since you were here, and my old eyes are of little service now."

"Well, nursie, tomorrow will be my birthday, and you are to come to dinner with me. Then I'll read to you if you wish."

"The precious child," said the old woman, "to think of a poor old nurse!"

"Good-by, nursie! I am not through inviting my friends

yet." Beckoning to Ann, Florie walked on a few doors farther and stopped at another home. A weak-looking child not much older than Florie came to the door with a crying baby in her arms.

"Why, Florie," the child exclaimed, "who ever would have thought of seeing you!"

"Where is your mother, Amy?"

"She is washing. The baby is so cross I can't do anything with him. I could not go to church last week because he was not well."

"Do you think your mother will let you come and have dinner with me tomorrow? It's my birthday."

By this time the woman appeared, and Florie asked: "Please, may Amy come to my house tomorrow afternoon? It will be my birthday. We are in the same Sunday school class, and I should like to have her."

"Certainly, miss; I have no objections." The mother and child both seemed happier to have Florie call.

"Where next?" Ann inquired.

"To Mrs. White's," said Florie. "I'm going to ask her to bring little deaf-and-dumb Tommy."

Florie made her errand known to Mrs. White, and left, saying: "Bring him at three o'clock tomorrow, please."

"Now for home!" said Florie. She ran to her room the moment she arrived and wrote this little note: "Florie Swift sends her compliments to Mrs. Swift, and would be pleased to have her company tomorrow afternoon."

"Ann, please take this to mamma, and wait for an answer."

Ann soon returned with a small piece of paper, on which was written: "Mrs. Swift accepts with pleasure the invitation for tomorrow afternoon."

The next day was bright and clear, and as three o'clock drew near, Florie began to arrange her table for the guests on the green lawn. A large dish of strawberries stood in the center, on one side a large cake, and on the other a plate of biscuits. A small bouquet of choice flowers stood by each plate.

"Your company is coming," said Ann, who was helping Miss Florie.

Sure enough, there was old nurse with her walking stick, and Jamie on the shoemaker's back. Blind Mary was the next to come, and soon Amy and little mute Tommy appeared. Seating old nurse in a large chair brought out especially for her, Florie put the rest of her guests on her right and left. Mary smelled the flowers, and was delighted with them. Mrs. Swift now came into the yard, looking somewhat astonished at the company. She greeted each one pleasantly, and sat at the head of the table.

When dinner was over, Mrs. Swift invited everyone to the parlor, where she played and sang for them. Each one had a bouquet to take home, and when they left they said, "Thank you," over and over.

When they were alone, Mrs. Swift asked Florie why she had invited these friends to her party.

"Mother, our teacher told us last Sunday that God said, 'Feed the hungry, lead the lame, and help the needy,' or something like that. Did I do right, mother?"

"Yes, daughter. I'm happy that you thought of others. He who gives to the poor lends to the Lord."

The Hard Way

"FRANK, I have one more errand for you; then you may go and play the rest of the afternoon."

"Yes, father, thanks. What is it you want me to do?"

Frank's father went behind the counter and drew out a little drawer. The man handed his son a silver dollar and said: "You may carry this to Widow Boardman. Be careful not to lose it."

"I'll be careful," promised Frank, and then went out the door.

It was the first day of vacation. The boy felt happy as he trudged along the road. He was thinking of the good days ahead—two weeks and no school! Perhaps the pleasant day, the fresh air, and the sunlight had something to do with making him happy. Something else helped to make Frank happy, although he was not thinking about it. He had tried his best to do right. It makes a wonderful difference when we know we are doing our best.

Mrs. Boardman lived some distance up the road. Frank had already passed the schoolhouse, and the little pond, and was passing the willow grove, when suddenly he decided to make a whistle to blow along the way. So, putting the dollar in his jacket pocket, he climbed over the fence and cut several willow twigs. He went along with the twigs in his hand, until he reached a log lying on a grass plot by the roadside. Here he sat down and made two whistles. They sounded wonderful to Frank's ears.

As he shut the widow's gate, Frank put his hand in his

pocket to take out the dollar, so that he might have it
ready to hand her when she came to the door. It was not
there. Thinking he had felt in the wrong pocket, he put
his hand in the other, fully expecting to feel the dollar between his fingers. *It was not there.*

Frank felt alarmed. Could he have lost it? He searched
carefully in every pocket, but the dollar was lost. He turned
around and went slowly back, looking carefully along the
road for the lost dollar. He searched around the log, in the
willow grove, by the roadside, every step of the way, but no
dollar was to be seen. He went over the road again with no
better success. At length he sat down upon the log to con-
sider what he should do.

The dollar was lost, there was no doubt of that. His
father had told him to be careful, and he had not been.
Now what should he do? His first thought was to go back
to the store and tell his father all about it. This would be
the right way; but he disliked to go, for he knew his father
would blame him for his carelessness.

Frank decided he would not go to his father then. He
would go and play with the boys awhile. Perhaps his
father would never know. At any rate he would not tell
him at once. So he got up from the log and walked slowly
toward the schoolhouse playground. Soon he was playing
with the boys.

In the evening Frank went home and sat down at the
supper table with the family. Soon after the blessing had
been said, while his brothers and sisters were talking with
each other about what they had been doing through the day,
father turned to him and said: "O Frank, did you carry the
dollar?"

"Yes, sir," answered Frank promptly.

The question was asked so suddenly that he had no time to make up his mind what to answer. He felt less like telling the truth than he had at first. It seemed too hard. He thought to take the easier way by answering "Yes." The easier way! Poor boy, he had not learned yet that it was the hard way.

Soon after supper Frank went upstairs to bed. When he said his evening prayer he did not feel that God was listening to him, and he passed a restless night.

In the morning he woke up to find the sun shining into his room. Leaping out of bed in high spirits, he began to dress. Suddenly he thought of the lost dollar, and this blotted out all his happy feelings.

The day went by slowly. Frank was troubled by the fear that father would find out about the lost dollar; yet he found it harder every hour to make up his mind to tell what had happened.

In the evening Frank could endure it no longer. The easy way had indeed become the hard way. While sitting in the front room he made up his mind to go and tell the matter. He started toward the study, where his father was. Every step in the right direction gave him new strength. He opened the study door and came to the table where his father sat writing.

"Well, Frank," father said kindly, "what is it?"

"O father," said the boy, but he could not go on. He bowed his head upon the table and sobbed.

In a few minutes Frank raised his head, and began again: "I want to tell you father"—but it was too much.

"Wait a minute, Frank. Let me tell you first," said father. "You want to tell me that you did not carry the dollar to Mrs. Boardman, that you lost it on the way, that last night you told a lie about it, that you felt wretched all the time. You wanted to tell me, but you did not dare. Is that it?"

"Yes, sir," sobbed Frank.

"You wanted to take a way easier than the right way, yet you have found it a great deal harder."

Frank knew that was true. He saw that he might have spared himself a great deal of uneasiness and sorrow by choosing the right way.

To help Frank remember, it was decided he should earn a dollar as soon as he could and take it to Mrs. Boardman. Frank set about earning his dollar, and before vacation was over, he carried it with a light heart to Mrs. Boardman.

The strangest part of the whole matter was that while Frank was returning from Mrs. Boardman's his shoe struck something hard; he looked down and saw the dollar he had lost!

Rose's Revenge

"BERTIE, here's your hat again tossed down behind the couch on the porch, instead of being hung up in the closet. Soon you would have called the family to help you look for it. Come and pick it up. I am going to require you to stay indoors all day the next time your hat is out of place. Remember."

Bertie's mother spoke emphatically. Bertie, a little sheepishly, said to himself: "I had better try to remember. Mother means it; she doesn't often speak so seriously."

The boy was in the children's room, busy painting with his new box of colors. Rose, his little sister, stood by, watching him with admiring eyes. It was fun for a while; but Bertie tired of it by and by, and leaned back in his chair, wondering what to do next. Presently a bright thought struck him, and he jumped up.

"Rose, you put away those things for me, won't you?" he asked. "I haven't time."

"Where are you going all of a sudden?" asked Rose, beginning to pick up the paint brushes and color box.

"Oh, out with my sled! I promised Jimmy Lane and Ned Wheeler to go coasting with them this morning. I forgot about it until this minute. I wonder where my hat is."

"O Bertie, may I go with you?" begged Rose. "I'll clean this all up for you. I won't be a minute. Mother said I might go with you the next time you went to the hill, if you'd take care of me. You will, won't you, Bertie?"

"Not this time," answered her brother, looking under

"Oh, boy," cried Bertie, jumping with delight, "the Brown's big sleigh! Think, Rose! Buffalo robes and bells!" Then Bertie remembered that his hat was lost!

chairs and tables for his hat. "Do you suppose a fellow wants to be bothered with a girl to take care of when he's going in for fun?"

"I think you might take me," persisted Rose. "The other boys take their sisters, and I haven't had a good ride all winter. Please, Bertie. I'll help you find your hat."

"Thanks, but I've found it myself. For a wonder, it was on the hatrack." Before Rose could put in another word, Bertie was off.

Poor Rose stood looking after him blankly for a moment. Then her face grew hot with anger. "He's a selfish boy," she said angrily, "and I know what I'll do."

Now, Rose didn't know exactly what she would do,

and by the time her brother came in to dinner, she had quite forgiven him. She remembered it again the next day, though, when mother, coming into the children's room, said: "Quick, children, get ready. Mrs. Brown has called to offer me a sleigh ride, and she says there is room enough for you. But hurry, the horses mustn't stand waiting in the cold."

"Oh, boy," cried Bertie, jumping up in delight. "The Browns' big sleigh! Think, Rose! Buffalo robes, and bells! Where in the world is that hat now?"

Rose was putting on her woolen jacket and getting her mittens and her hat. She was so busy she had not heard what her brother was saying; and he, disgusted at seeing her all ready, broke out in loud reproach.

"Yes, that's all you care, you selfish thing," he cried. "You're all ready, and you don't care whether I have to stay or not. I haven't had a good sleigh ride this whole winter. Where is that old hat?"

"I know where his hat is. I saw it fall behind the big chest a little while ago. I suppose if I didn't tell him, and made him stay home, it would be my revenge." Rose looked a little triumphant at her brother. Then she said: "Hurry on your coat and mittens. I'll find your hat." She ran to the chest, and came back as her mother appeared at the door.

Bertie looked a little sheepish as he followed his mother and sister out to the sleigh, and all he said was a hurried whisper: "You're a good girl, Rose." He said to himself, quite in earnest this time, that he had been a selfish, careless boy, and that this sort of thing had to be changed right now. Rose's "revenge" had worked.

Aunt Jane's Party

ALMOST everyone in town knew Aunt Jane. She was aunt to a dozen or more boys and girls in particular, and to all the rest in general. Aunt Jane bestowed a great deal of care and thought on her relatives, and all the time they did not claim was devoted to helping others. It was a wonder to all how she accomplished so much. She kept house by herself in a quiet way, yet not exactly alone. Children and poor persons not happy at home sought her home, where they were sure to receive sympathy in all their troubles.

Well, I had almost forgotten that I was going to tell you about Aunt Jane's party.

She was always doing "something queer," as the people called it; but, for all that, everyone loved her and approved of everything she did. Now, the party was to be on Wednesday afternoon, and the invitations were given out several days before.

Some children who had no brothers or sisters felt quite slighted because they were not invited, for she invited by pairs, but only two from any one family, even if there were a dozen children. The children's parents thought it a strange thing to do, but said there was probably a reason, if Aunt Jane did it that way.

The long-expected day arrived. There were about twenty boys and girls at the party. They played games and had exciting contests.

After the refreshments, the children were invited to look at colored pictures through a viewer that enlarged the pictures. Only one child could see the pictures at a time. The first boy rushed eagerly toward the chair, fearing that someone would be there before him. The rough push he gave his sister hurt her, and she, provoked by it, pulled his hair.

The last to see the pictures were a brother and sister named Charles and Mary Ellis, ten and eight years old. Charles and his sister had waited patiently until the last. Then, seeing that it was their turn, Charles placed the chair in the best light, and said: "Now, Mary, it is your turn."

"Oh, no!" she said. "You look first. I am in no hurry."

Someone by their side said: "You may take it home and look at it as long as you like."

Looking up, the brother and sister saw Aunt Jane smiling at them. "I had intended to give a present to every brother and sister who did not get provoked with each other," she said; "but I have watched all of you, and have noticed that Charles and Mary Ellis are the only ones who have not shown signs of selfishness. This present is a reward for your kindness. Do you think I have given it to the two who are most deserving?"

"Yes, yes!" they all exclaimed. We hope they resolved to treat each other more kindly in future.

Into the Sunshine

"I WISH father would come home." The voice of the boy who said this had a troubled tone.

"Your father will be angry," said Aunt Phoebe, who was sitting in the room reading a book.

Richard raised himself from the sofa where he had been for half an hour, and with a touch of indignation in his voice, answered: "He'll be sorry, not angry. Father never gets angry."

"That's father, now!" He started up after the lapse of nearly ten minutes, as the sound of a bell reached his ear, and went to the door. He came slowly back, saying with a disappointed air: "It wasn't father. I wonder what keeps him so late. Oh, I wish he would come!"

"You seem anxious to get into deeper trouble," remarked the aunt, who had been in the house for a week only, and who was not sympathetic toward children.

"I believe, Aunt Phoebe, that you would like to see me whipped," said the boy, a little indignant; "but you won't."

"I must confess," replied the aunt, "that I think a little whipping would not be out of place. If you were my child, I am quite sure you would not escape."

"I am not your child, and I do not want to be. Father is good, and he loves me."

Again the bell rang, and again the boy left the sofa and went to the door.

"It's father!" he exclaimed.

"Ah, Richard!" was the kindly greeting, as Mr. Gordon

took the hand of his boy. "But what is the matter, my son? You don't look happy."

"Won't you come in here?" Richard drew his father into the library. Mr. Gordon sat down, still holding Richard's hand.

"You are in trouble, my son. What has happened?"

Richard's eyes filled with tears as he looked into his father's face. He tried to answer, but his lips quivered. Then he opened the door of a glass case and brought out the fragments of a broken statue which had been sent home only the day before. A frown came over Mr. Gordon's face as Richard set the pieces on a table.

"Who did this, my son?" was asked in an even voice.

"I threw my ball in the room once—only once, in forgetfulness." The poor boy's tones were husky and tremulous.

For a little while Mr. Gordon sat controlling himself and collecting his disturbed thoughts. Then he said cheerfully: "What is done, Richard, can't be helped. Put the broken pieces away. You have had trouble enough about it, I can see. I will not add a word to increase your distress."

"Oh, father!" And the boy threw his arms about his father's neck. "You are so good."

Five minutes later Richard entered the sitting room with his father. Aunt Phoebe looked up expecting to see two shadowed faces, but she did not find them. She was puzzled.

"That was very unfortunate," she said a little while after Mr. Gordon came in. "It was such an exquisite work of art. It is hopelessly ruined. I think Richard was a naughty boy."

"We have settled that, Aunt Phoebe," was the mild, but firm, answer of Mr. Gordon. "It is one of our rules in this house to *get into the sunshine as soon as possible.*"

Into the sunshine as quickly as possible! It's the best way!

Lily May's "Good Time"

"OH, DEAR! I wish I didn't have to mind mother. When I grow up and have a little girl, I'll let her do as she pleases. If she wants to go out to play after school, I won't make her come straight home."

So said Lily May as she walked slowly toward school, feeling much abused because mother thought it was not safe for a child who had just recovered from a fever, to play in the brook that afternoon.

At home, mother said to herself: "I wonder if it would be safe for Lily May to play in the water. I was sorry to disappoint her, but I was afraid she would get cold. I think that tomorrow I shall give her permission to do as she pleases. That will let her see if she is as happy as she thinks she will be."

That night Lily May came home and began to fret. "I know I would not have caught cold playing in the brook," she whined.

"Tomorrow you may do as you please in everything, Lily May," said mother.

"Do you really mean it?" exclaimed the girl joyfully.

"Certainly, my dear."

"Oh, won't I have a wonderful time! How I wish it were tomorrow now!"

The next morning after breakfast Lily May said: "Now, mamma, I don't believe I'll go to school today."

"Do as you please, my dear," said mother.

The girl went outdoors, and presently mother saw her

(49)

Lily May sat in the swing wishing she had more to do. She decided to go into the house and get a piece of cake. Somehow it didn't taste good.

swinging under the tree. In about half an hour she re-appeared, saying: "Mother, will you please give me something to eat?"

"Take anything you please," replied her mother. Lily May helped herself to a generous slice of fruit cake.

The morning hours dragged heavily for the girl. She tried one pastime after another, but found that play alone was not desirable. In fact, she would have been glad if her mother had given her some work; but she was too proud to acknowledge herself wrong and ask for some task.

After dinner she said: "I believe I'll go to school this afternoon, but don't be worried if I don't get home until suppertime."

"Very well," said her mother, smiling quietly.

After school, some of Lily May's friends said: "Come with us, Lily May, and wade in the brook; you don't know what fun we have."

The girl hesitated. Something within her told her she ought not to go; but, stifling the little voice, she hurried after the girls. Somehow she did not enjoy the wading as much as she had expected. The girls spattered water over her; and at last, one of the larger girls, for the fun of it, pushed her down into the water. Then she began to cry, and her classmates called her a crybaby and told her to run home to her mother. This she did willingly; and just before dark her mother saw a forlorn-looking little girl, her wet clothes hanging closely about her, coming to the front door.

What do you suppose her mother did then? Did she refuse to help her? Did she say that Lily May had done as she pleased all day, and might do as she pleased about getting warm and dry? No, indeed; she helped the girl change her wet clothes for dry ones, and gave her a hot supper. Then she wrapped her up warm and cozy in her bed. As mother was bending over her for a good-night kiss, Lily May threw her arms around her neck, and said: "I think it was good of God to give little girls mothers to take care of them, for they know so much more than children."

Paul's Canary

"I DON'T see why I was made this way. I was such a sickly baby, everyone thought I would die. I wish I had—" Paul paused when he thought of his weary mother and how happy he would be when she came home.

He was crouching on a seat by the one window in the room, looking out at the tall buildings and the wet boards of the near-by houses. Sometimes, leaning out far enough, he could see the paved yard, with its pile of boxes and rubbish.

Paul was far from strong. His deformed legs could hardly carry him about.

"I'm of no use at all," cried Paul. "I'm only a trouble to mother. I don't believe there is another creature in the world as helpless as I am."

As he spoke, a gust of wind shook the loose sash and blew the rain furiously against the panes. The blinds next door rattled as the storm seemed to gather force and beat against the window. Then Paul started forward with breathless curiosity to examine a little dripping object that the wind had blown onto the ledge by the window. It was a bird, apparently helpless, scarcely fluttering as it clung feebly to the stone.

"Oh, poor bird, I'll bring you in!" cried Paul. Opening the window, he gently reached out his hand. In his haste he forgot to fasten up the sash and it pressed heavily on his shoulders. The wind blew his hair into his eyes and the rain drenched him; but he did not worry about this, his only thought was for the weak creature he hoped to rescue. The

Paul watched the bird flutter on the window ledge. It seemed that the storm was determined to snatch the bird away before he could lift the window.

storm seemed determined to snatch the bird away before he could reach it. At last, however, he gathered the wet bird in his hands and drew it into the room. Before he thought of changing his clothes, he wiped, stroked, and blew the bird's feathers, trying to fan the spark of life.

The bird lay in Paul's hands hardly moving. Slowly it began to revive and to pick at its feathers. Then Paul considered himself. He had no other pants and jacket, so he wrapped himself in a blanket, taking his new pet under its folds. In the warmth and darkness, it slept. Paul, with a new feeling of content, watched it until he, too, fell asleep. When his mother came home, she feared he was sick; but on turning back the blanket, she was greeted by a lively chirp from the bird, which was now dry and comfortable. The little fellow displayed a handsome suit of black and yellow. One of his wings was injured, and parts of two toes were gone; but he was bright and chirpy and very hungry.

"Why, Paul, where did this come from?"

Paul related the rescue, and ended by asking: "Isn't he pretty?"

"Yes; but he must have some seed. I'll see if they won't give me a bit downstairs," said mother.

Soon she returned with some birdseed, and, to Paul's satisfaction, the bird began to eat. A little water in a cup served him for drink, and he slept on a stick that Paul balanced between two chairs.

In the days that followed, Paul no longer complained or felt discouraged while his mother was absent earning their living. Pet, as he named the bird, was his playmate. Paul taught the canary to take seed from his lips, to lie dead at a word of command, and to pull his master's hair or eyebrows to get attention.

Now, the birdseed that mother had borrowed soon disappeared, and Paul wondered how to get more. It would not be fair to use mother's money. Could not he earn some? He thought and thought.

The window next to his room jutted out so that he often saw Mary sitting at her work. She was sorry for the lame boy, and spoke to him. He made up his mind that she might help him. One day, as she sat plying her nimble fingers, he called: "Mary, please. What do you call your work?"

She looked up and smiled. "Tatting."

"Is it hard to do?"

"Oh, no! It's easy; you could learn it."

"Could I make enough to buy Pet some seed?"

"Why, yes; do you want me to teach you?"

"Oh, do!" cried Paul eagerly.

"I'll come in tonight."

So she did. Paul's fingers were straight and strong and he had a will to learn. Pet tried to investigate the process, pulling the thread; but Paul sent him to bed, and worked away until he could make the stitches as Mary did.

"I'll sell it for you at the same place I take mine; and if you are industrious, you'll more than buy Pet's seed—a cage, too, perhaps."

"Oh, he doesn't want a cage."

After that, Paul sat in his window as busy as anyone. He was happy over his work; and when a few pennies were left over after buying the seed, and he could buy some fruit for mother's lunch, he was as happy as any other child. Mother declared that her son was growing straighter, and someday he would be strong and would take care of her.

Some months after Paul rescued Pet, he was wakened by feeling something on his face. As he opened his eyes, he felt Pet pulling his hair with such strong tugs that it was far from pleasant. The morning light was stealing into the room, its gray cold making everything look dim and strange. Pet pulled and tugged at his master's hair.

"It's not day," said Paul, trying to send Pet away; but the bird would not go. Finally, Paul had to get up and put the canary on his perch. As his hand touched the wall, he noticed it was quite hot. Pet refused to stay on his perch, clinging instead to his master's shoulder.

"Mother," cried Paul, "mother, wake up!"

His mother was weary, and made no reply. As Paul listened, he heard the roar of fire and smelled the smoke.

Springing on his mother's bed, he wakened her and told her of the danger. She ran to the hall and aroused their neighbors; and in a moment the large house, with its many families, was in confusion. The next room was in flames. The fire had started from some clothes that were hung too near the stove; and if it had not been for Pet's alarm it would have been serious. As it was, the firemen came and soon extinguished it, though Paul's room was badly burned and he was obliged to sit with Mary the next day.

Everyone in the house came to see the lame boy and the canary that had saved their property and perhaps their lives. Paul was praised; and so many people wanted Pet, that Paul was afraid they would carry him off. Then came the man who owned the house, and he told Paul that he had saved him many thousand dollars, and asked him what he would like to have. Paul's face flushed, and then he timidly said: "Some crutches, sir, so that I can go into the street."

"You shall have them," replied the man. Paul's mother received a sewing machine, so that she did not need to go out to work; and Pet had a comfortable cage to sleep in, and all the seed he could eat.

Bertha's Queer Graveyard

BERTHA DICKINSON was a decided enemy of tobacco. She used to say she hated it. Now hate is a strong word, I know. My mother has often said to me, "My dear, you must hate nothing but sin;" and I never use the word without thinking of her advice. But I think, as Bertha did, that it is quite proper to say hate in speaking of tobacco, for it is a poison, and it injures more people than most folks are willing to believe. And then it is so nasty! There, that is another word my mother never liked to hear me use. She said it isn't a "pretty word." But I think it fits tobacco; and Bertha always thought so, too.

Bertha was a queer child. She never acted like other children, but had a way all her own, which sometimes made folks laugh, and sometimes cry, and always made them shake their heads, and say: "What an odd little girl Bertha Dickinson is!"

She took a notion into her head one day that she would have a little graveyard all her own. There was a piece of ground in the garden behind the house where nothing was planted. A long row of blackberry bushes hid this corner from the house, and she used to go down there to play. It was one day after she had been to visit Thomas Hill, the village undertaker, that she got the idea of having the graveyard. She went straight off to the woods, and brought home four pretty little trees, which she planted in the four corners of the lot she had chosen; and then, thinking it best to get permission to use the ground, she went to find her father.

"Daddy! Daddy!" she called aloud, as he and several men were threshing grain in the barn. "Will you give me the northwest corner of the garden?"

"The what, child?"

"The northwest corner of the old garden. It is bounded on the north by the old apple tree, east by the walk, south by the blackberry bushes, and west by the sweet-corn field."

There was a general laugh at the conclusion of this speech. Mother and Hapsey came out to see what was the matter.

"You needn't make fun of me," exclaimed Bertha. "I tried to be particular, so I could save you the trouble of going to see the spot."

"Bertha wants me to deed her the northwest corner of the garden, mother," said Mr. Dickinson. "Are you ready to sign the papers?"

"What do you want it for, my dear?" asked mother. "Are you going to build a dollhouse?" Her mother knew that that particular spot was her little girl's favorite resort. She was quite unprepared for the answer, and for the roar of laughter, which was repeated as the child looked up and replied:

"I want it for a graveyard, mother."

When father had recovered the power of speech, he pursued his inquiries further. "What are you going to bury, dear?"

Quick as a flash of light, Bertha picked up her father's pipe, which lay on the wooden bench by the door. "This first," said she, and off she ran.

So quick was her motion and the words that accompanied it, that no one saw what she had done. But when the day's work was finished, and the farmer was ready for his evening

As Bertha sat on her father's knee, she said: "I didn't want you to die as Mr. Thurston did." Her father smiled and agreed to leave the pipe buried.

smoke, the pipe was missing and could not be found.

"Where is my pipe? Who has seen my pipe?" shouted father in no very pleasant tones.

"I buried it, daddy, in my new graveyard," said the child coolly. "Come and see."

The heavy steps of the tired man and the light trip-trip of the little girl's feet fell together on the garden walk as they proceeded to the northwest corner of the garden, where Bertha pointed to a neat little mound. At the head of it was placed a bit of shingle with the inscription:

"HERE LIES
MY FATHER'S PIPE.
REST FOREVER."

The astonished parent was at a loss for words. He did not know whether to laugh or to be angry. Finally he concluded to do neither, but to try to get at the child's meaning in all this. So, sitting down on an overturned wheelbarrow, he took Bertha on his knees and began to question her. "Why did you do this, child?"

"Because, daddy, I didn't want you to die, as Mr. Thurston did. It's a fact, daddy," seeing a smile gathering on his face. "I heard Dr. Bell say so when we were coming from the funeral. Miss Stevens asked him what was wrong with Mr. Thurston, and Dr. Bell said: 'Pipe, Miss Stevens, pipe. He smoked himself out of this world and into—well, Miss Stevens, I can't say exactly where he has gone. If folks get so used to their pipes here in this world, I don't see what they're going to do in the other. It seems to me they'll want to keep up the smoking. I'm almost sure they can't do it in heaven, for you know, Miss Stevens, heaven is a clean place, and there is not going to be anything there that defiles.' So, daddy, I thought I'd dig a grave and bury the old pipe. You won't dig it up, will you?"

The farmer held his peace for a few minutes. Then he said slowly, but firmly: "No, Bertha, your father is no grave robber. I shall miss the old pipe; but I suppose I must say about it as we do about everything that's put in the grave, 'Thy will be done.'"

"That's good," said the child, with a kiss.

"Was that what you wanted this great graveyard for?" asked father, smiling again, and seeking to divert the conversation which he feared might get beyond his depth. "Was it only to bury that old pipe?"

"No, indeed," exclaimed Bertha earnestly. "I'm going to bury other things here, too. I expect I shall have a funeral almost every day. I'm going to bury old Auntie's snuff next."

"How will you get it?"

"Oh, I'll get it! I'll manage, daddy. And then there are Joe's cigarettes, and Uncle Ned's cigars."

Bertha proved to be a busy little undertaker, and before the week had passed more than a dozen items had been buried in the new cemetery. The graves were all made evenly, side by side, exactly the same size, nicely rounded and turfed. At the head of each was a tiny board on which was printed some simple epitaph. These headboards cost the girl a great deal of time and labor. On one was: "Auntie's Snuffbox. Closed Forever." On another: "Joe Tanner's cigarettes. Lost to view." On the next: "Cyrus Ball's Cigar. Burned out."

The northwest corner lot was finally full. More than sixty neat little graves were there in rows. The apple tree spread a friendly shade over the spot, and the blackberries ripened beside them; and many and many a visitor was taken slyly down the garden walk to see Bertha's graveyard. But the best part was that for every mound in that quiet spot, there stood a man or woman redeemed from an evil habit, a living monument above it, and all alike bearing testimony to the faithfulness and perseverance of a girl who loved purity and good health.

The Boy Who Took a Boarder

ONCE upon a time, about two hundred and fifty years ago, a boy stood at the door of a palace in Florence, Italy. He was a kitchen boy in the household of a rich and mighty official. He was twelve years old, and his name was Thomas.

Suddenly he felt a tap on his shoulder. He turned around and said in great astonishment: "What! Is that you, Peter? What has brought you to Florence? How are all the people in Cortona?"

"They are all well," answered Peter, who likewise was a boy of twelve. "But I've left them for good. I want to be a painter. I've come to Florence to learn to paint. They say there's a school here where people are taught."

"But have you any money?" asked Thomas.

"Not a penny."

"Then you can't be an artist. You had better be a servant in the kitchen with me, here in the palace. You will be sure of something to eat, at least."

"Do you get enough to eat?" asked the other boy reflectively.

"Plenty, more than enough."

"I don't want to be a servant; I want to paint," said Peter. "But I'll tell you what we'll do. As you have more than you need to eat, you take me to board, and when I'm a grown-up painter, I'll settle the bill."

"Agreed!" said Thomas, after a moment's thought. "I can manage it. Come upstairs to the garret where I sleep, and I'll bring you some dinner by and by."

So the two boys went up to the little room among the chimney pots where Thomas slept. It was a small room, and the only furniture in it was an old straw mattress and two rickety chairs. The walls were whitewashed.

Now the food was good and plentiful, for when Thomas went down into the kitchen and foraged, he found abundance that the cook had carelessly discarded. Peter enjoyed the meal, and told Thomas that he felt as if he could fly to the moon.

"So far, so good," said he; "but, Thomas, I can't be a painter without paper and pencils and brushes and colors. Haven't you any money?"

"No," said Thomas, "and I don't know how to get any. I shall receive no wages for three years."

"Then I can't be a painter, after all," said Peter mournfully.

"I'll tell you what," suggested Thomas. "I'll get some charcoal down in the kitchen, and you can draw pictures on the wall."

Then Peter set resolutely to work, and drew so many figures of men and women and birds and trees and animals and flowers, that before long the walls were covered with pictures.

At last, one happy day, Thomas came into possession of a small piece of money. I don't know where he got it, but he was much too honest a boy to take money that did not belong to him.

You may be sure there was joy in the little room up among the chimney pots. Now Peter could have pencils and paper, and other things artists need. By this time the boy had learned to take walks every morning. He wandered about Florence, drawing everything he saw: the pictures in the churches, the fronts of the old palaces, the statues in the square, or the outlines of the hills. Then, when it became too dark to work any longer, Peter would go home and find his dinner tucked away under the old bed, where Thomas had put it, not so much to hide it as to keep it warm.

Things went on in this way for two years. None of the servants knew that Thomas kept a boarder, or if they did know it, they good-naturedly shut their eyes. The cook sometimes said that Thomas ate a good deal for a lad of his size.

One day the owner of the palace decided to repair it. He went all over the house in company with an architect and poked into places he had not visited for years. At last he reached the garret, and there he stumbled right into Thomas's room.

"Why, how's this?" he cried, astonished at the drawings in the little room. "Have we an artist among us? Who occupies this room?"

"The kitchen boy, Thomas, sir."

"A kitchen boy! So great a genius must not be neglected. Call the kitchen boy."

Thomas came in fear and trembling. He had never been in his employer's presence before. He looked at the charcoal drawings on the wall and then into the face of the great man.

"Thomas, you are no longer a kitchen boy," said the official kindly.

Poor Thomas thought he was dismissed from service, and then what would become of Peter?

"Don't send me away!" he cried. "I have nowhere to go, and Peter will starve. He wants to be a painter so much!"

"Who is Peter?"

"He is a boy from Cortona who boards with me. He drew

those pictures on the wall, and he will die if he cannot be a painter."

"Where is he now?"

"He is wandering about the streets to find something to draw. He goes out every day."

"When he returns, Thomas, bring him to me. Such a genius should not be allowed to live in a garret."

Strange to say, Peter did not come back to his room that night. One week, two weeks went by, and still nothing was heard of him. At the end of that time a search was made and at last he was found. It seems he had fallen deeply in love with one of Raphael's pictures that was exhibited in a public building, and had asked permission to copy it. The men in charge, charmed with his youth and talent, had readily consented. They had given him food and a place to stay.

Thanks to the interest the rich official took in him, Peter was admitted to the best school of painting in Florence. As for Thomas, he had masters to instruct him in all the learning of the day.

Fifty years later, two old men were living together in one of the most beautiful houses in Florence. One of them was called Peter of Cortona; and the people said of him: "He is the greatest painter of our time." The other was called Thomas; and all they said of him was: "Happy is the man who has him for a friend."

He was the kind boy who took care of his friend.

One Minute More

ON A bright sunny day while Ned sat at the breakfast table he tried to get his mother or sister to tell him where they were all going.

"I'm as much in the dark as you are," said Carolyn. "I think that mother was afraid I would let out the secret, for she sometimes calls me her little chatterbox. We're to be ready at ten o'clock sharp."

"Well, I suppose we'll know in a few hours. Look, here comes Charley Wood. I promised to show him something in my workshop." Away ran Ned.

The boys played together until after nine o'clock; and then, instead of going directly to the house, to be on hand promptly at ten o'clock, Ned thought: "Oh, there's time enough for me to finish my kite."

Two or three times his eyes were upon his watch; but there were a few minutes to spare, he thought. When he looked again, he was startled to find that it was three minutes past ten. By the time he had his hat and rushed to the front room, he was five minutes late, and no one was there.

He could not believe that his mother would disappoint him for such a little delay, so he called for Carolyn. Then he ran to his mother's room to see if she were there, then out the front door; but no one was to be seen.

"Why did mother not tell me where she was going? Then I might have overtaken her. Now I don't know in which direction to go," mumbled Ned.

It was because of this that his mother had not told Ned

Charley and Ned worked on the kite in Ned's shop, and the minutes flew
by so fast that the next time Ned looked at his watch it was after ten.

where she was going. He was in the habit of trying to make
up for lost time by hurrying at the last minute.

Mrs. Gray had planned a visit to her sister, who lived on
a farm. Ned and Carolyn had once visited there and had
a grand time with their cousins. They played in the hayloft,
searched for eggs, helped feed the cattle, and rode the horses
to water. They often begged mother to take them again; but
she had many home cares and could not get away.

Poor Ned! When he found his mother and sister gone,
he was a disappointed boy. Half ashamed to have Jane, the
maid, see his tears or know how miserable he was, he went
back to his play. He knew that if his mother returned,
Carolyn would be sure to run out to the playhouse in search

of him, so he stayed out there by himself until dinnertime.

Jane called Ned to dinner. She had lived in the Gray home a long time and knew Ned's one failing. She had promised Mrs. Gray not to tell him where his mother and sister had gone, until dinnertime. The woman saw the boy with sad, downcast face enter the dining room. Seeing the table set for only one person, Ned was surprised, for his mother rarely stayed away all day.

The boy sat down to his lonely meal, and when Jane came in with a piece of pie, he asked why his mother was not home to dinner.

"Oh, Ned," she replied, "your mother won't be back today, or tomorrow either—no, not until Monday morning. She and Carolyn have gone to visit your Aunt Mary."

This was too much for the youth. Dropping knife and fork, he rushed upstairs to his room, where he flung himself on the bed and cried bitterly.

When he had recovered from the first burst of tears, he remembered his mother's request "not to forget," that she should expect him "in the front room at ten o'clock precisely." Now he understood that she must have started with Carolyn to the station at the very moment the clock hands pointed to the hour. It was a good lesson. He knew his mother had not meant to be cruel to him, and he resolved to improve in promptness.

It was with bright, sunny face, from which all sadness had vanished, that Ned met his mother and sister when they reached home Monday morning. Mrs. Gray saw at once that the hard lesson she had been obliged to teach him had not been in vain.

Making Up

MRS. MORTON had noticed for several mornings that something had gone wrong with little Donna May. The child seemed as happy as usual at the breakfast table; but when schooltime drew near, she became restless. She took her hat and coat long before the hour and stationed herself at the window, looking up the street, as if waiting; yet when the time came, she went reluctantly, as though she had no heart to go.

When she came home at noon she was sadder than when she went.

"What grieves my little daughter?" asked her mother, as she came into the room.

"Oh, mother!" said Donna May, crying outright at a kind word. "You don't know!"

"But I want to know," said Mrs. Morton. "Perhaps I can help you."

"Nobody can help me," said Donna May. "Alice Barnes and I—we've always been friends, and now she's mad at me."

"What makes you think so?" asked her mother.

"Oh, I know! She always used to call for me mornings, and we were together at recess and everywhere. I wouldn't believe it for the longest time; but it's a week since she called for me, and she keeps away from me all the time."

"Now that I know what Alice has done, dear, can you think of anything you did?"

"Why, mother! No, indeed, I don't need to think. I thought too much of Alice." May cried again.

"There, my dear, don't cry. You must find out why she keeps away from you. Very likely there is something that you never thought of."

"I don't want to ask her, mother. It's her fault, and she ought to come to me."

"I fear your pride is stronger than your love for Alice," said mother. She was brushing Donna May's hair as she spoke, and she stooped to give the girl's forehead a loving kiss. Donna May knew that her mother was right, for she went straight to Alice when she saw her on the sidewalk after school, and said: "Alice Barnes, why are you mad at me?"

"I shouldn't think you would ask me, Donna May Morton," replied Alice, "when you've said such unkind things about me."

"No such thing!" said May indignantly.

"Donna May," said Alice, looking as solemn as her round, rosy face would let her, "didn't I hear you, with my own ears, telling Bess Porter that I was the most mischievous little thing you ever saw?"

Donna May looked blank for a moment, then burst into a laugh. Alice turned angrily away; but her friend caught her by the arm, and, choking down her laughter, said: "Alice, don't you know I named my new canary bird after you? I was telling Bess about her, and how she tore her paper to pieces and scattered her seeds all over the floor."

Alice stared and drew a long breath. Donna May's eyes twinkled again and both girls forgot their grievances in a peal of hearty laughter.

"There, Alice," said Donna May afterward, "if we ever misunderstand each other again, let's speak about it at once. Perhaps it will be something as funny as this."

Joe Green's Lunch

IT WAS a little past noon, and a merry group of boys were seated on the grass under the trees that shaded the academy playgrounds. A little later they would be scattered in every direction at their play, but first they must attend to the contents of the well-filled pails and baskets of lunch.

"I should like to know," said Howard Colby, "why Joe Green never comes out here to eat his dinner with the rest of us. He always sneaks off somewhere until we get through."

"Guess he brings so many goodies he is afraid we will rob him," said another.

"Pooh!" said Will Brown, throwing himself back upon the grass; "more likely he doesn't bring anything at all. I heard my father say the family is badly pinched since Mr. Green was killed. Mother said she didn't pity them, for folks had no business to be poor and proud."

"Well," said Sam Merrill, "I know that Mary Green asked my mother to let her have some sewing to do; but then, folks do that sometimes who aren't poor."

"And Joe is wearing patched pants," said Howard Colby.

"I tell you what, boys," said Will Brown, "let's watch tomorrow to see what the fellow does bring. You know he is always in his seat by the time the first bell rings, and we can get a peep into his basket before roll call."

The boys agreed to this, all but Ned Collins, who had sat quietly eating his dinner. He had taken no part in the conversation. Now he simply remarked, as he brushed the crumbs from his lap: "I can't see what fun there will be in that, and it looks mean and sneaking to me. I'm sure it's none of your business what Joe brings for dinner or where he goes to eat it."

"You're always nicey nice, Ned Collins," said Will Brown contemptuously.

Ned could not bear to be laughed at. His eyes flashed for a minute, and then he sprang up, shouting: "Hurrah, boys, for football!" In five minutes the whole playground was in an uproar of fun and frolic.

The next morning at the first stroke of the bell a half dozen roguish faces peeped into the classroom. Sure enough, there was Joe Green, busily plying his pencil over the problems of the algebra lesson. It was but the work of an instant to hurry into the cloakroom, and soon the whole group were pressing around Will Brown, as he held the mysterious basket in his hand. Among them, in spite of the remonstrance of yesterday, was Ned Collins.

"It's big enough to hold a day's rations for a regiment," said Harry Forbes, as Will pulled out a nice white napkin. Next came a whole newspaper—a large one, too; and then, in the bottom of the basket, was one cold potato. That was all. Will held it up with a comical grimace, and the boys laughed loudly.

"See here," said Howard, "let's throw it away, and fill the basket with coal. It will be such fun to see him open it!"

The boys agreed, and the basket was soon filled, and the napkin placed carefully on the top. Before the bell rang, they were on their way to class.

Ned Collins was the last one to leave the room. No sooner did the last head disappear, than, quick as a flash, he emptied the coal into the box again, replaced the paper, and half filled the basket, large as it was, with the contents of the bright tin pail that Aunt Sally delighted to store with dainties for his dinner. Ned was in his seat almost as soon as the rest, and all through the forenoon he looked and felt as guilty as the others, as he saw the sly looks and winks they exchanged. Noon came, and there was the usual rush to the cloakroom for dinner baskets; but instead of going out to the yard, the boys lingered about the door and the hall. Straight by them marched Ned Collins, his pail under his arm.

"Hello, Ned!" said Sam Merrill. "Where are you going now?"

"Home," said Ned, laughing. "I saw Aunt Sally making some extra goodies to eat this morning, and they can't cheat me out of my share."

"Ask me to go, too," shouted Howard Colby. At that moment the boys spied Joe Green carrying his basket into the schoolroom.

"I should think he'd suspect something," whispered Will Brown; "that coal must be awful heavy."

Joe disappeared into the schoolroom, and the curious eyes that peeped through the crack of the door were soon rewarded by seeing him open his basket.

"Hope his dinner won't lie hard on his stomach," whispered Howard Colby. But apparently Joe only wished to get his paper to read, for he took it by the corner, and pulled; but it stuck fast. He looked in with surprise, and then took out, in a sort of bewildered way, a couple of Aunt Sally's fat sandwiches, one of the delicious round pies he had so often seen in Ned's hands, a bottle of milk, and some nuts and raisins. It was a dinner fit for a king, so Joe thought, and so did the boys as they peeped from their hiding place. But Joe did not offer to taste it; he only sat there and looked at it. Then he laid his head on his desk; and Freddy Wilson, one of the smaller of the boys, whispered, "I guess he's praying," so they all stole away to the playground, without speaking a word.

"That's some of Ned Collins's work," said Will Brown, after a while. "It's just like him."

"I'm glad of it, anyway," said Sam Merrill. "I've felt mean all forenoon. The Greens are not to blame for having only cold potatoes to eat, and I don't wonder Joe didn't want all us fellows to know it." Will Brown began to feel uncomfortable.

"Father says Mr. Green was a brave man," said Sam Merrill, "and that he wouldn't have been killed, if he hadn't thought of everyone else before himself."

"I tell you what," said good-natured Tom Granger, "I move that we give three cheers to Ned Collins."

The boys sprang to their feet, and, swinging their caps in the air, gave three hearty cheers for Ned Collins. Even Will Brown joined in the chorus, with a loud "hurrah."

Later that day, Sam Merrill explained the whole matter to Ned; but he only replied: "I've often heard Aunt Sally say it's poor fun that must be earned by hurting someone's feelings."

The Conductor's Mistake

THE train was waiting at a station of one of our Western railroads. The baggagemaster was busy with his checks. Men, women, and children were rushing for the cars, anxious to get seats before the locomotive pulled away.

A man, carelessly dressed, was standing on the station platform, seemingly giving little attention to what was going on. It was easy to see that he was lame; and at a hasty glance, one might have supposed that he was a man of neither wealth nor influence.

The conductor gave him a contemptuous look, and slapping him familiarly on the shoulder, called out: "Hello, Limpy! Better get aboard, or the train will leave you behind."

The man made no reply. As the train started to move, the man climbed on the last car and walked quietly in and took a seat.

The train had gone a few miles when the conductor appeared at the door of the car where our friend was sitting. Passing along taking tickets, he soon discovered him. "Your ticket, quick!"

"I don't pay," replied the lame man quietly.

"Don't pay?"

"No, sir."

"We'll see about that. I shall put you off at the next station." And he seized his valise.

"Better not be so rough, young man," returned the stranger.

The conductor seized the bag, but then put it down and went on collecting fares. In a few minutes he learned to his sorrow who the old man was.

The conductor released the bag for a moment, and seeing that he could do no more then, passed on to collect the fare from the other passengers. As he stopped at a seat a few paces off, a man who had heard the conversation, asked: "Do you know who that man is to whom you were speaking?"

"No, sir."

"That is Peter Warburton, the president of the road."

"Are you sure?" asked the conductor, trying to conceal his worry.

"I know him."

The color rose in the young man's face, but with strong effort he controlled himself and went on collecting fares as usual.

Meanwhile Mr. Warburton sat quietly in his seat. None of those near him could interpret the expression of his face, nor tell what his next movement would be. He could get even if he chose. He could tell the directors the truth, and the young man would be fired. Would he do it? Those who sat near him waited curiously to see what would happen.

Presently the conductor came back. He walked up to Mr. Warburton's seat and took his books from his pocket, the bank bills and tickets he had collected, and laid them beside Mr. Warburton.

"I resign my place, sir," he said.

The president looked over the accounts for a moment, and then, motioning him into the vacant seat beside him, said: "Sit down. I want to talk to you."

When the young man sat down, the president spoke to him in an undertone: "My young friend, I have no wish for revenge. You have been imprudent. Your manner would have been injurious to the company if I had been a passenger. I could fire you, but I will not. In the future, remember to be polite to all you meet. You cannot judge a man by the coat he wears, and the poorest should be treated with kindness. Take up your books, sir. If you change your conduct, nothing that has happened will injure you."

Burned Without Fire

JOHNNY found a big brass button and set to work shining it on a piece of woolen cloth. "Isn't it bright?" he said, after working awhile. "Just like gold!"

He rubbed away again as hard as he could, then brushed the button across the back of his hand to wipe off some chalk dust. I had told him to put chalk on the cloth to brighten the button quicker.

"Ow!" he cried, dropping the button.

"What's the matter?"

"It's hot."

"Hot!" echoed Mary, laying down her book. "How can it be hot?"

"I don't know," said Johnny, "but it burned me."

"Nonsense!" replied Mary, picking up the button. "It's cold."

"It may be now," Johnny admitted; "but it was hot— warm, anyway."

"What a silly boy! You imagined it."

"I didn't," retorted Johnny.

Seeing that they were likely to do as many older people have done, dispute about a matter that neither understood, I took the button and rubbed it smartly on my coat sleeve and then put it to Mary's cheek.

"There!" exclaimed Johnny, as Mary cried "Oh!" and put her hand to her face.

"I shouldn't have thought your arm could make it so warm," she said.

I rubbed the button on the tablecloth, and placed it once more against her cheek, saying: "It couldn't have been my arm that warmed it this time."

"Of course not," observed Johnny.

"What did warm it?" Mary asked, her interest fully awakened.

"That's a good puzzle for you two to work at," I said. "Don't rub the button on the furniture, for it might scratch that; but you can try anything else."

Mary and Johnny worked for a long time, and still they were puzzled.

"Maybe the heat comes from our fingers," Mary suggested at last.

I put a stick through the eye of the button, so that it could be held without touching the hand. Then I rubbed it on the carpet, and it was as hot as ever.

"I guess it's the rubbing," said Johnny.

"A good guess indeed, for that is precisely where the heat comes from," I replied. "The simple fact that heat comes from rubbing is perhaps enough for you to know about right now."

"I thought heat always came from fire," said Mary, "or else from the sun."

"There are other sources of heat," I replied; "our bodies, for instance. We keep warm when out of the sunshine and away from the fire."

"I never thought of that," said Mary.

"Do you remember the day the masons were pouring water on a pile of quicklime to make mortar for the new house over the way? The lime hissed and crackled, sending up clouds of steam. I have a piece of quicklime here. See, when I pour water on it, how it drinks up the water and grows hot. I saw a wagon loaded with lime set on fire once by a shower of rain."

"Fred told me about that, but I didn't believe him. Who'd expect fire from water?"

"Get me a small piece of ice, and I'll show you how even that may kindle a fire."

While Mary was getting the ice, I took from my cabinet a small bottle with a metal bead at the bottom.

"Is it lead?" asked Johnny, when I showed it to him.

"It is potassium," I said. "I'm going to set a little piece of it afire with the ice Mary has brought. There."

"Isn't it splendid!" cried Mary, as the metal flashed into flame.

"You can do anything, can't you?" said Johnny admiringly. His confidence in my ability is something frightful. Really, if I were to tell him I could set the moon afire, I think he'd believe me.

"No, Johnny," I replied; "there are very few things that I can do, as you will discover in time. But now, while we are talking of heat, let me show you another way of warming things. Please fetch me that old piece of iron in the garage, Mary, while Johnny brings my hammer."

When the materials were ready, I said: "Now watch me while I pound this piece of lead, and be ready to put your finger on it when I stop."

"Does the pounding heat it?"

"It does. I have seen a blacksmith take a piece of cold iron and hammer it on a cold anvil with a cold hammer until it was hot enough to set wood afire."

"But we are a long way from Johnny's button. Can you think of any other time you have seen things heated by rubbing?"

"We rub our hands when they are cold," Mary said, seeing Fred go through these motions when coming in from outdoors.

"I've read of savages' making fire by rubbing sticks together," Fred continued.

"They have several ways of doing it—or rather, different savages have different ways. One of the simplest is to rub one stick in a groove in another, rubbing briskly and bearing down hard. There is a bit of soft pine board that I made to experiment with, the other day. See! When I plow this stick up and down in the groove, the fine wood dust that gathers at the bottom begins to smoke a little and turns black. By working long enough and fast enough, I could set the dust on fire; but it is too tiresome when a match will do as well. We get our fire by rubbing, too, only we use something that kindles quicker than wood. A single scratch on some rough surface develops heat enough to light it."

"What is it?" Mary asked.

"Phosphorus. I have some in this bottle. You rub the button, Johnny, while I take some of the phosphorus out on the point of my knife. Now touch it with the button. See! It is hot enough to set the phosphorus afire. We might light our fires that way; but it is more convenient to put the phosphorus on the end of a stick, and mix it with something to keep it from catching fire too easily. All we have to do is to rub the phosphorus point against anything rough. The friction heats it, and it takes fire.

"Did you ever hear of the traveler who was stopped by some barbarous people who knew nothing of matches? They would not let him go through their country, and while they were debating whether to kill him or send him back, he took a match from his pocket, struck it against his boot, and lighted it. To his surprise the people ran off to the village. After a while the chief man came back humbly, bringing loads of presents. He begged the traveler to go on his way in peace."

"What was the reason?"

"They had seen him draw fire from his foot, as they thought, and were afraid that he was a god who might burn them all up if they offended him."

The Temptation

TWO boys, both about fifteen years of age, were employed as clerks in a large grocery store. Walter Hyde was the son of an invalid widow, and his earnings were her only means of support. Andrew Strong was the eldest son of a mechanic who had quite a large family depending upon him for their daily bread.

Both the boys were capable and industrious; both were members of the temperance club that had been started in their church. They had but lately been employed in business.

Walter and Andrew were good friends; but they had not long been employed in the store before they learned that Mr. Bates, the proprietor, retailed alcoholic drinks.

The two boys talked together upon the wisdom of remaining at a place where liquor was sold. They had nothing to do with the sale of the liquor, but they wondered if they should work where it was sold.

"Let us talk with our folks at home," said Walter, "they will know best. I shall do what my mother says."

"I'll ask my father and mother," said Andrew. "I don't know whether they will think that I should leave, but I know they will hesitate to have me lose my job."

"Mother," said Walter Hyde, seating himself beside her easy chair, "did you know that Mr. Bates sells liquor?"

"Why, no, my son," said Mrs. Hyde, with a startled movement; "does he?"

"Yes. I did not know it for a fact until today. What do you think about my staying there? I don't have anything to do with the liquor department, but it doesn't seem exactly right to stay where it is sold."

For a moment the mother did not answer. Poverty is a hard thing to battle with, and Mrs. Hyde knew only too well what must follow the loss of her son's job. But as she pondered, there came to her mind the memory of a boy she had known in girlhood; a brave, high-spirited lad with the promise of as noble a manhood as lay before her own son. How little a thing had wrecked his hopes and brought him to a drunkard's grave.

"Lead us not into temptation." When could those words be more fitly uttered than now?

"My son, let us pray together," said this Christian mother. Together they knelt in prayer in the cheerful firelight.

"I can answer you now, Walter. I would rather starve than have you exposed to such temptations. You may tell Mr. Bates in the morning that you cannot work for him any longer."

In his home that evening Andrew Strong asked the same question of his parents.

"You say you don't have anything to do with the liquor?" questioned Mr. Strong.

"No, sir; but I am right where it is all the time. I can't help that, if I stay there."

"If we were able to get along without your wages, I wouldn't have you remain another day; but I have so many mouths to feed, and our rent is coming due. If you leave there you may not get another job in a long time. What do you think, Anna," he inquired of his wife; "had the boy better leave?"

Mrs. Strong was worried about money, so she suggested a compromise. "Let him stay a little while," she said, "until

Walter resigned, but Andrew stayed on at the store. After a time he began to taste, and then to drink, alcoholic liquor. This led to trouble.

we get the rent paid, and meanwhile look up a new job for him. We won't have him remain longer than necessary."

The next day Walter Hyde resigned his position. Walter, when he found himself out of employment, did not sit down and fold his hands in discouragement, but went about looking for another job. He picked up a little work here and there. At last a gentleman, struck by his frank, manly countenance, and learning something of his history, interested himself in the boy's behalf and got him a job as clerk in a large manufacturing establishment, a far better position than he had before.

Andrew Strong remained in the store of Mr. Bates. "It was only for a little while," said his father and mother. They intended to find him another job as soon as possible. His father made inquiries to that effect whenever he thought it advisable, but nothing turned up. At first no apparent evils resulted from his stay. Familiarity with a danger causes it to seem less dangerous, so the family finally ceased to feel troubled regarding the temptations that surrounded Andrew.

For a long time Andrew remembered his pledge and was careful to avoid the liquor department of the grocery. But as the days passed and he grew accustomed to the sight and smell of liquor, occasionally he tasted intoxicating drinks. He no longer attended the meetings of the temperance club, for after he broke his pledge he felt that he had no right to be there. He did not have the courage and resolution to confess his wrongdoing and change his ways.

Twenty years passed. In one of our large manufacturing cities, as the wealthy owner of nearly half the mills in the place was walking along the street one day, he saw a man by the roadside drunk. He stopped to see if he could not do something for the poor fellow.

"Do you know this man?" he inquired of a mill superintendent who was passing by.

"No. He is a stranger here. He came to me yesterday morning to work in the mill. I hired him, and then he told me he had been out of work so long that he had been unable to get anything to eat. I paid him for yesterday's work to help him get something to eat; but it looks as if he spent it for liquor."

"What did he tell you his name was?" inquired the factory owner.

"Andrew Strong," was the answer.

"Is it possible!" The gentleman looked long and earnestly at the tramp and then said: "Yes, it must be he." Then, turning to the superintendent, he said: "Mr. Horton, if you will help me carry this man to my house, I will do you a good turn some day."

Mr. Horton looked surprised, but he did as his employer requested.

When Andrew Strong awoke from his drunken slumber he found himself in a well-furnished room surrounded by many conveniences. Beside him sat a gentleman whom he could not recall having ever seen before.

"Where am I? What does this mean?" he demanded as his senses returned to him. "Why am I here?"

"Andrew Strong," said the stranger, "do you remember me?"

"No, I never saw you before," was the answer.

"You are mistaken. You and I were once old friends. Don't you remember Walter Hyde, who used to work with you in the store?"

"Yes, yes," was the answer, "but are you Walter?"

"I am the same boy who talked with you about leaving the store because of the liquor sold there."

The man looked with bleary eyes into the face of his companion, and after a long pause said: "Then I suppose you are the Hyde that owns all these factories."

A pause, and then came a groan from the poor drunkard. "Oh! that my father and mother had kept me from that liquor house. That is where I went down. If I had left the place as you did, I might now be an honored and re-spected man."

"My poor friend, do not despair," said Walter Hyde. "It is not yet too late for you to reform. I will help you."

He did help him. Andrew Strong became a man re-spected by his fellows and a blessing to society.

The Two Gardens

"ARTHUR, will you lend me your knife to sharpen my pencil?" asked Mary Green of her brother, who was sitting at the opposite side of the table.

Arthur drew the knife from his pocket, and pushed it rudely toward her, saying, at the same time: "Now don't cut your fingers off."

The knife fell to the floor and Mary had trouble finding it, but her brother made no offer of assistance. He seemed engrossed in his geography lesson. At length he closed his books, exclaiming: "Well, I'm glad that lesson is learned."

"Now will you please show me how to do this example before you begin to study again?" asked Mary. She had been puzzling over a question in subtraction.

"You are big enough to do your homework, I should think," was the answer. "Let me see. What, this simple question? You must be stupid if you cannot do that. However, I suppose I must help you. Give me the pencil."

The problem was soon explained to Mary's satisfaction. Several hints given her as to those which followed prevented further difficulty. Arthur did not mean to be unkind to his sister; he loved to help her, though his manner seemed harsh and cross. Presently father sat down at the table where the children were studying.

"You are impolite, my son," he said.

"I cannot always think about manners," replied Arthur, rather rudely.

"Yet they are of great consequence, Arthur. A person

Mary and Arthur put aside their studies and listened as father told them that their manners were of great importance in making a success in life.

whose intentions are really good, and who desires to be of use to his fellow beings, will hurt his chances of usefulness by unkind manners."

"If we do what is right, father, I shouldn't think it matters how we do it."

"You are mistaken, Arthur. It makes a great deal of difference. This morning I visited a poor woman in the neighborhood. I couldn't help her much, but for the little that I gave her she appeared deeply grateful. Finding that she had formerly been employed as a laundress by a man whose office is near mine, I asked why she did not apply to him for help. The tears came into her eyes as she replied: 'Indeed, sir, I know he is very kind, and he has helped me before when things went hard; but he has such a harsh way of speaking. A penny with kindness is worth a dollar from those who hurt our hearts.'

"Now, my son, I know this man to be a man of principle, but he has acquired a harsh, repulsive manner, which hides his good qualities. When you were helping your sister this evening you were unkind."

"But I did not feel unkind, father. Are not our feelings of more consequence than our manners?"

"Both are important, Arthur. It seems to me that kind feelings should produce kind manners."

Arthur thought but little more of what his father had said. He did not improve his manners, and his playfellows said of him: "Arthur Green is a goodhearted boy, but so rude and cross in his manners. One would suppose he is angry even when he is doing a favor."

Mr. Green had recently moved his family to a country home. Both Arthur and Mary liked the fresh air and the green fields. They asked their father to give them each a piece of ground for a garden and to show them how to prepare it for planting. This he agreed to do. Arthur did the most difficult work, but Mary was always ready to help. The brother and sister were fond of flowers, and looked forward to the time when they would be able to gather armfuls from their own garden. Their father gave them seeds and plants, and he helped them in the planting. Before many days little green leaves began to peep above the ground, and as the season advanced all the plants seemed to flourish.

"The seeds father gave me must have been different from those he gave you," said Arthur to his sister, as they were weeding their gardens one day.

"I suppose he thought we would not want to have the same kinds of flowers," replied Mary.

"No, of course not," agreed Arthur; "but I don't like the looks of my plants as well as I do yours. The leaves are coarser, and the buds don't look as if they would make pretty flowers."

Arthur grew more and more dissatisfied as Mary's plants were covered with beautiful blossoms, while his own had either no flowers at all, or were pale and small. Having had no experience in gardening, he could not imagine the reason and complained to his father.

"I am sorry that you are not satisfied with your garden, my son," was the reply. "The seeds that I gave you were the seeds of vegetables. When I last looked at them, they seemed to be growing fine."

"Vegetables, father!" exclaimed Arthur. "I wanted flowers. I didn't want to have a vegetable garden."

"I didn't suppose you would care for flowers, Arthur. Of what use are they?"

"They may not be of much use, father; but they are beautiful. We like to look at them and to have them to give to our friends. Are not things useful which give pleasure?"

"I think so, my son, but you seemed to have a different opinion. In preparing your garden, I avoided giving you those plants which possess any beauty, even as you avoid cultivating what is beautiful and pleasing in your manners."

Arthur was silent. He was struck with the truth of his father's words. At length he said: "Well, father, I will take good care of my vegetable garden this year. Every time I visit it I'll think of what you said. When you see better words and manners in me will you give me a garden that is beautiful as well as useful?"

"I will, son."

When another summer came, there had been a change in Arthur. The real kindness of his heart shone forth in his agreeable manners toward all around him. Flowers were blooming in his garden, and his father said: "These represent kindness and love."

Always the Bible

"ALWAYS the Bible!" said Horace Cooper to his sister. "Aren't you tired of it?"

"Almost," said Marian, laughing; "but still not *quite* as indignant as a boy not far off."

"Here we came down into the country to enjoy ourselves for the holidays, and instead of that—"

"Now, Horace," interrupted his sister, "I am sure you have had lots of fun. There were rides and uncle's amusing stories of his travels. There were luncheons in the arbor and walks with Charles and Fanny. Come, now, I can't let you find fault with *everything*."

"Perhaps not; but remember that on the excursion we had to sing a hymn under the trees, and to listen to a psalm."

"Yes, the sixty-fifth," said Marian.

"Well, and then in those stories of travel, uncle brings the same Book forward constantly. In the arbor don't we sing hymns and read verse by verse. In our walks, Charles and Fanny learn memory verses and ask us to do the same."

"So it is," returned the sister. "I confess that at first the reading and prayers, morning and evening, appeared strange; but now I begin to like it. Anyway, I do not wish myself back at Uncle Herbert's as I did the first day or two."

Horace and Marian Cooper were orphans under the guardianship of the "Uncle Herbert" of whom we have heard them speak. When about ten years of age, they had been sent to boarding schools in the city. A few summers

That evening in the cheerful drawing room, Mr. Loxley began the story. Everyone looked up and smiled when he began by saying: "When I was a boy—"

after this we find them spending a vacation with "Uncle Loxley down in Cornwall," as Horace always called him.

A beautiful place was Fernley, as Mr. Loxley's place was called. The house had ivied walls, surrounded by gardens.

That evening in the cheerful drawing room at Fernley, Mrs. Loxley, Marian, Fanny, Charles, and Horace awaited the arrival of Mr. Loxley. Charles has discovered that there is a particularly interesting story for this evening, and even Master Horace was ready to listen and applaud. At length Mr. Loxley entered and took his armchair.

"Bertha," he said, addressing his wife, "I have a long letter to read to you. What is the matter, Fanny? How crestfallen you look, my child! and Marian, too!"

"O father, it's our story; we thought you would begin now."

"Oh, I see,"—there was a merry twinkle in Mr. Loxley's eye as Charles explained the downcast looks. "I see," continued the man with assumed gravity, "the letter will have the goodness to wait awhile."

Everyone smiled assent. Mr. Loxley cleared his throat and the "story" began. "When I was a boy—"

Everyone looked up.

"Well, then, I will choose some less antiquated beginning. The snow lay thick on Salisbury Plain as I rode home from school on the top of a stagecoach. Dark and dismal was the night, not a star to be seen. It was such a night as would suit the adventurous Master Horace yonder. The coach was heavily laden, and the horses—we had six of them—could scarcely drag us over the road.

"Presently the guard whispered to a gentleman at his side: 'Shan't get through this without some mishap;' and, at the same instant, down went the coach in the deep snow. The passengers dismounted, the horses struggled nobly, still it was evident that, without more horses, the coach could not move. A conference was held, and it was resolved that the larger number of the passengers, with the guard, should proceed to the nearest village and send help immediately."

"But how could they find the way?"

"Hush, I am going to tell you. There was one man on the coach who knew 'every step of the road,' and, with a lantern in his hand, this man, looking at the waymarks which he so well knew, was to guide us to the village."

"That was great," said Horace, who was all attention.

"This man was called Guidewell, and an honest guide he was. In our company, hastening with us over Salisbury Plain, was a self-conceited man, Mr. Careless I shall call him, who never appealed to our guide. As for the rest of us, we followed Mr. Guidewell carefully. By and by Mr. Careless said: 'Why do you trust to this man? I believe I know the best way after all.'

" 'Have you ever been on this road before?' I asked, with schoolboy forwardness.

" 'Why, not exactly; but I'm tired of hearing your constant appeals to Mr. Guidewell. I wonder if you will join me to strike off to the left and find the way as best we can.' "

"Oh, how foolish!" cried Fanny.

"That's silly," cried Horace. "When one has a guide who knows the way, surely no one would go off alone and be lost!"

Mr. Loxley looked grave. "In vain we argued with him; in vain we called our guide and questioned him as to the safety of such a course. Mr. Guidewell asserted that the path which he pointed out was the only safe course; but Mr. Careless shook himself away, saying, 'Always this Guidewell, I'm tired of him.' "

"Uncle, the man must have been mad."

"Was he ever heard from again?" asked Charles.

Mr. Loxley still looked grave. "You are wrong," he said; "for, happily, some of the words which Mr. Guidewell uttered made a deep impression on the mind of Careless, and before he had walked a hundred yards, he returned and acknowledged his mistakes."

All brightened at this unexpected conclusion, and during the next five minutes the children expressed their opinions of the story.

"But father hasn't finished," suggested Fanny presently.

"Well, perhaps I should tell you that we reached the village in safety, and that the coach was soon out of the hole. The part of my story I want to impress on your memories is the adventure of Mr. Careless."

There was a pause, and then Mr. Loxley, in his kindest manner, said: "Horace, my boy, come here." Horace obeyed. "And Marian." Marian came to the other side. Their uncle took a hand of each.

"This morning," said Mr. Loxley, "I accidentally heard these words in my garden: 'Always the Bible; aren't you tired of it?'

"I stayed to hear no more; but I told you this story to help you. If a man refuse to be guided by the Bible, if he choose *his own path*, what shall be said of him? Will not the words uttered a moment ago express it: 'How foolish'?"

The brother and sister chose God's word for their guide, and the motto of their lives was: *"Always the Bible."*

We invite you to view the complete
selection of titles we publish at:
www.TEACHServices.com

scan with your mobile
device to go directly
to our website

Please write or email us your praises, reactions, or
thoughts about this or any other book we publish at:

TEACH Services, Inc.
P U B L I S H I N G
www.TEACHServices.com • (800) 367-1844

P.O. Box 954
Ringgold, GA 30736

Info@TEACHServices.com

TEACH Services, Inc., titles may be purchased in bulk
for educational, business, fund-raising, or sales
promotional use. For information, please e-mail:

BulkSales@TEACHServices.com

Finally if you are interested in seeing
your own book in print, please contact us at

publishing@TEACHServices.com

We would be happy to review your manuscript for free.